OCEAN OF BONES

Shane Gericke

Damnonii Publishing

To my sisters,
Marianne Taylor and Diana Gericke,
the real angels in my life

"The evening sky was streaked with purple, the color of torn plums, and a light rain had started to fall . . ."

Dear Readers,

A decade ago, I died from heartbreak.

I came back to life in 2025 thanks to crime novelist James Lee Burke, who pulled me out of the grave into which I'd fallen the day I buried my wife, Jerrle. Thing is, I didn't know Burke was helping me get my mojo back. He didn't either. That miracle was arranged from above by Jerrle, who decided I needed an angel to rekindle my passion for writing and for life and chose Burke for the robe and wings.

I guess I'd better explain.

I'd been writing professionally since high school; first for newspapers, then crime novels. My wife of forty years, Jerrle, loved my work because she loved to read. We cracked open books every night before sleeping, reading aloud passages that made us laugh or gasp. The one topping this letter was a gasp—of admiration. It was Burke's opening sentence for *The Neon Rain*, the 1987 crime thriller that introduced his Dave Robicheaux character to the world. "The color of torn plums" grabs me as much now as it did then.

When Jerrle became terminal with metastatic breast cancer, she vowed to stay alive long enough to attend the publication-day party we'd planned to launch my fourth novel, *The Fury*. "I'll get a fire department ambulance if that's what it takes," I vowed. "Only if the Dalmatian comes too," she said. We would hold the party at our hometown Anderson's Bookshop in Naperville, Illinois, where I'd launched my first three books. The date was September 4, 2015, her 60th birthday, which wasn't coincidental because my favorite reader wanted a books-and-birthday party with family and friends.

She died four days short. I buried her one day short.

And now, the party.

Deep in my bones I wanted to cancel. But since Jerrle had insisted the show must go on, my sisters, friends, and I turned that event into book launch, birthday party, and celebration of her life. I staggered through the evening with what my sister Diana described as a thousand-yard stare, glad I kept my promise but nonetheless reeling like a prizefighter who'd taken one too many shots to the face.

That last one put me down for the count.

Jerrle's final squeak for air ended our reading ritual. I stopped caring even remotely about writing and books, which I'd so loved until she got sick. I quit reading fiction. I ghosted friends. I wandered our house alone and dazed, every inch a reminder of something. Everything I'd enjoyed about life became dull as road gravel. I thought the mourning would pass, but one year became two, five, nine. I'd fallen into the purgatory Jerrle feared most: alive, but not living.

Then, her brother Jess Miller gifted me a first edition of *A Private Cathedral* by James Lee Burke. JLB was a favorite of all three of us, so Jess thought I'd enjoy revisiting old friends. After he left, I prepared to slip it into the Cupboard of Unread Children in which I kept novels I'd purchased to support writer friends—nothing says "love ya" like a book sale royalty—but couldn't bear to read. For some reason, I decided to open this one before putting it away . . .

> *"No sooner had he finished his prayer than he felt his head begin to swell as though all the blood remaining in his body had filled his cranium and was beginning to boil, squeezing his eyes from their sockets, bursting his eardrums, setting his brain alight."*

"Damn, that's nice," I muttered. Encouraged by the sudden tingles in my writing fingers, I read it again, then grabbed *The Tin Roof Blowdown*, Burke's deep dive into the evil that bestrode New Orleans after Hurricane Katrina:

"The pistol shots were loud and sharp. Andre took one round in the neck and two in the head, both of them as hot as wasp stings. Later that night, his body roped to another person's and a chain of cinder blocks, he awoke to starlight just as someone rolled him over a gunwale into water that smelled of diesel fuel and fish spawn."

My mind drifted back to the pleasure Jerrle and I took in reciting such passages to each other. I recalled the thrill I got crafting just one perfect sentence in *The Fury*, which I'm now reimagining and rewriting into a global thriller for future release:

"The duct-taped Buick swam north on Rush Street, hunting whores like a lesser white shark."

I wondered if I could write like that again. *Yes. I want to. And I will.*

I was back.

But why those two passages? I don't know. Why did they exhume my buried mojo? I have no clue. The glory of reading is just that—you never know what will change your life. Those passages did. They helped me connect with Jerrle's spirit. And thus ended a decade of drowning in the bleak and chilly grave-water of heartbreak.

No surprise, because her will is as strong in the afterlife as it was here. Five weeks before she died, she announced, "You're going to keep writing when I'm gone."

"What if I don't want to?"

"I'm dying and tragic, so you have no choice."

I rolled my eyes. "Seriously? You're playing the death card?"

"I'll do whatever it takes to keep you writing," she said.

"What's the point?" I scoffed. "Nobody cares about my little crime stories."

At this point of end stage, she barely had the energy to dunk a tea bag. Yet she managed to shake her head violently. "I care," she rasped. "Crime fiction tells the truth about people at their worst. You do that better than anyone I know. The world needs to read you. Promise me you'll keep writing." She fell back panting from the effort but continued to stare from the hospital bed that hospice installed next to our marriage bed so I could read aloud to her when she could no longer see. Yes, metastatic cancer is that kind of monster. "I asked all my friends to look after you when I'm gone."

"I know. It's nice."

"If they tell me you're not writing, I'll come back and haunt you."

When I read those random passages, I remembered how much she loved Burke's work—Clete Purcel and his porkpie hat was her favorite character in all crime fiction. She decided she could trust Burke to convince me "it's time to start living, podno," and arranged it through spirits and angels and passages in his books.

My first flush of newfound creativity was selling my landscape photographs through the online art gallery Fine Art America. I wrote a piece of flash fiction for the literary magazine *Dribble Drabble,* and it was accepted in twenty-four hours. I wrote a poem that didn't suck, won six international photography awards, and thought about the best way to get back on the fiction horse that threw me.

This story is that horse, and we're going for a ride.

James Lee Burke is closing in on his fiftieth bestselling novel. We've never met, but his characters—Louisiana Sheriff's Deputy Dave Robicheaux, best friend and "podno" Clete Purcel, daughter Alafair Burke, and Dave's father, Aldous "Big Aldous" Robicheaux—are good friends to tens of millions of readers. The online literary magazine *CrimeReads* describes Dave Robicheaux as "an amalgamation of swashbuckling detective, political activist, and Catholic theologian. A literary emblem of Raymond Chandler's theory that the crime investigator is modernity's substitute for the medieval knight, the protagonist of most of James Lee Burke's novels is a flawed and complex hero whose struggles against the mafia, serial killers, child predators, and bigots and bullies of fascistic ideologies magnify into stories with implications so large they feel borderline cosmic."

I wrote *Ocean of Bones* as an allegory for my lost decade: drowning emotionally in a watery grave, drifting as the world swirled by overhead, then being reunited with life by Jerrle and books. Accordingly, the story is about an oil worker blown off a doomed rig in the Gulf of Mexico, never found, and presumed dead. Years later, the oil gods decide it's time to repair the circle of life they so callously broke and choose a pair of wisecracking treasure hunters to do the job. How those sub-borne hunters pull it off is for your reading pleasure.

Thank you, Jerrle Miller Gericke. Thank you, James Lee Burke. Thank you, family, friends, and readers. Without you, I'd still be in the briny deep.

It's nice to breathe fresh air.

With gratitude, Shane Gericke

1

T he rope was greasy with insects and sea slime. It smelled like an alligator pulped by a truck. Broussard, irritated, considered taking the tugboat back to New Orleans, where he could soothe his flambéed brain with beignets and hair of the dog, then return when the motorized crew lift was fixed. But Lucien and Marcus needed new school clothes, so getting fired as a no-show wasn't an option.

He sighed, spat on his hands, grabbed the twisted hemp, and climbed up the side of the oil rig. His boots skidded off the waterlogged algae, prompting flurries of French Cajun curses at whatever hoodoo had broken the winch that normally hoisted workers to the top. He collapsed onto the sun-fried deck.

"How we feeling today, Remy?" chirped his boss, whose name was Bagley.

"We feeling we throw you over that rail," Broussard panted. "If only we could move."

"Is God's wrath," Bagley said, "for what you done last night."

Broussard's grin showed clamshell teeth against his walnut-brown face, which was mapped with the folds of years working wind-blown oil platforms in the Gulf of Mexico. This rig was his latest, but it wouldn't be his last; not till his two sons were grown. "How many sheriffs they need this time?"

"Thirteen," Bagley grumbled, throwing up his hands. "All them deputies to haul one measly Cajun from a titty bar. What's this world coming to?" He squinted against the egg-yolk sun. "You cost me serious money, Knockout."

Broussard rubbed his knuckles. He loved to fight and was uncommonly good at it. Not enough to make a living as a boxer, but as a legend among the mosquito-bitten sheriff's deputies of southern Louisiana, nobody hit harder. When oil workers came ashore after months of forced temperance on the Gulf of Mexico—booze hounds died fast on a wave-tossed oil drilling platform—alcohol flowed and so did fists.

Oil and fighting were his only passions beyond his boys and his wife, Amélie, beautiful Amélie. She'd realize any day now the smooth-talking Houston oilman who'd lured her from her adoring husband's bed with promises of riches, excitement, and the golden calf of "the good life" was a hoodoo man. When he finally did her wrong, as hoodoo do, Amélie would run back into his arms and to the boys she'd abandoned for bright lights big city. Remy would forgive her those years away because he'd forgiven her the moment she'd left.

He touched his right temple and squinted at his reddened fingertip. Blood still wept into the bandage from the divot gouged by a deputy too scared to fight so he swung a pool cue. Deputies like to lay bets on how many of them would be required to wrestle Knockout Broussard into the drunk tank. They took their licks but admired him anyway—he let the deputies wail on him without complaint, and he never threw a sucker punch. The previous record to take him out of the fight was eleven. Last night, he'd kicked that up by two . . .

"That's why you made me climb the stink rope," Broussard said, realization dawning as he clambered to his feet. "You bet against me and lost."

"Payback's a bitch," Bagley said.

Fully unwound, the master of the oil rig's derrick crane towered over Bagley. "I ought to crush your grapes, Dirtbag."

Bagley stiffened at the hated nickname. "Call me that again and I'll put you on latrine duty with the coons," he said. "Scrubbing crusties ain't white man's work, but maybe you'd learn something from them boys about not sassing your betters."

Broussard hawked and spat over the guard rail. "Why you gotta call 'em that?"

"What, coons? Why not? You like jigaboos better?"

"They do a day's work like the rest of us poor slobs," Broussard said. "You got no call to piss in their cornflakes." He sighed, waved his hand. "But yeah, all right, you're the boss."

"See, you learned something." Bagley curled away to reply to a radio squawk. "Yep, he's aboard, get started." He turned back. "Most of us lost our bets."

"Not me," Pieton said as he ambled up. "I made a fortune."

"You're too loyal to your friend."

"Too loyal, yet rich too," Pieton said.

"You a damn good bud, Pie," Broussard said, patting the squat, bald mechanic.

Bagley stuffed chaw into his wide mouth. He looked like a pig gumming corncobs. "No way was you gonna skunk a dozen deputies, Knocks," he said. "Not humanly possible, so I put my money on eleven but . . . ah, hell and grits."

Broussard laughed. "I'll tell you how to win your money back, if you want."

"Be a fool not to," Bagley said. "But why would I trust you to tell me the truth?"

"You're the boss man. Helping you helps me, right?"

Bagley spat tobacco juice. A gooey bubble ran down the crease of his chin. "Well, my old pappy did say never look a gift horse in the mouth," he said. "Whaddaya got?"

"Next time we're in port, put your money on sixteen."

"You'll beat sixteen deputies? Are you kidding?" Pieton said, goggling.

"Sweet sixteen, Pie. Guaranteed. If all three of us bet everything down to our skivvies, we'll walk away kings."

Bagley's small eyes lit with greed. "Isn't life more fun on my good side, Knocks?" he said, slapping Broussard on the back.

"You said it, boss."

They paused for the clank and rumble of oil machinery coming alive. Soon, the gang would rattle chains and slop mud as the long steel snakes of the floating oil platform Happy Jack, the pride and joy of Derringer Oil, bit deep into the bottom of the Gulf of Mexico to suckle viscous black milk from Mother Earth. The sound gave Broussard a feeling of peace. If he was good at fighting, he was great at oil. Even Bagley agreed, though he'd admit it only when lit on moonshine. Broussard knew every gear, pipe, plank, and shaft on this offshore oil barge, what their mechanical songs meant, and when the orchestra was even a half-note sour.

"Let's get to work, boys," Bagley said, turning for the pump station.

Broussard grabbed Pieton's arm. "Bet fourteen, not sixteen. Screw Dirtbag." Pieton winked and headed for the derrick crane. Broussard pulled a rubber pouch from his pocket, fished out the pencil stub and oilcloth-wrapped notebook, and wrote to Lucien and Marcus: *My boss man made me climb a really long rope today. It smelled like a horse's butt. Not the boss, the rope, but come to think of it, Boss Bagley smells that way too.* Like everything he put on paper, this was in Cajun French, because to call his written English "indecipherable" was a kindness.

"Broussard!" Bagley hollered. "I pay you to sweat, not write."

"All right, boss, I'm get the git going, me," Broussard drawled in the Cajun patois that annoyed Bagley. He was on the rigs for months at a time to put food on the table back home, and he missed clowning around with the boys on his cypress-shaded property along a lazy, winding bayou on the fringes of Thibodaux, Louisiana, where mosquitos mimicked dive bombers and humidity bubbled like tar pits. He wrote these notes so one day they could read all about their father's adventures, though they'd have to learn Cajun French ...

He walked to the steel-pipe guard rail and checked the one-man escape pod chained to the side of the rig. He nodded with not a little pride because the idea for the floating pod was his. He'd built it from an oversized pipe he'd liberated from a passing garbage scow. The pipe was bronze because that held up best to salt water. He'd capped both ends, cut a manhole through the "roof" of the pipe, and welded a watertight hatch over the hole. He padded the interior with rubber in case waves knocked him around, then added a tank of compressed air, a jerrican of water, a lidded bucket for waste, and a rigid steel seat from a P-51 Mustang. When the rig dropped into the Gulf, he could bob along the surface with the hatch open, sipping moonshine like a dandy, or dog down the hatch during a storm, snuggling with the family mementos he kept in a watertight box that once held machine gun ammo. The pontoon assemblies he attached to the "bottom" of the pipe would keep him afloat till rescue.

The guys thought his pint-sized invention hilarious. "Hey, look, it's a Bug," they hooted as Broussard cut and welded, referring to that new Volkswagen Beetle car making waves in America. "Remy's stink bug!" But Derringer Oil was intrigued by the concept of individual escape pods and allowed Broussard to work on it whenever he was off the clock, so he adopted the gibe as the official name of his mighty mite. He slept in *Stink Bug* most summer nights to escape the goatish smell of sweaty men snoring in a barracks of bunk beds—er, "to gauge the human-factors efficiency of life pod design," as a visiting Coast Guard officer advised Broussard to add to his development notes. After the officer departed the rig, Broussard asked Pie what "development notes" were. Pie explained, and Broussard diligently wrote them in the back of the notebook he kept inside his work shirt.

Bagley was tapping his wristwatch, so Broussard ambled toward the bunkhouse, which occupied the ground floor of the platform's superstructure. Rig life contented him. It was filled with men who enjoyed their work—or at least didn't hate it. It let him and his pals make decent money, feast on hot chow and coffee around the clock, play cards and dice, and brag about their prowess with women and football, real or imagined. Doing well on the rigs and talking to his boys through his notebook made him realize he'd made something of his life after all. When his Amélie came home, life would be per—

He froze in mid-step and lowered his thick, shaggy curls toward the wood-plank deck, which was scoured white from sea salt, crude oil, chaw, spit, sun-fried bugs, and mud. He'd felt something. What, he wasn't sure: A hum? A whisper? It passed through his gnarled toes, then was gone, quick as it came, quiet as a cough in a cathedral.

"Did you feel that, boss?" he called out.

"Feel what?" Bagley said.

"A wiggle in the deck. Maybe a shake."

"The hell you talking about, Knocks?"

"There's a hoodoo in the water," Broussard said. He stood perfectly still in hopes of catching it on the rebound. He was a firm believer in the sprites, faeries, angels, and spirits who made life more interesting, if occasionally exasperating, by delivering messages and impressions from the afterlife. Angels were top shelf, as they were kind, good talkers, and let you try on their wings if you asked nicely. Hoodoos were the tricksters of the bunch, the cranky little gnomes who'd stick out their legs and trip you just for laughs. If you sensed one's presence, it was best to find it fast and kick it away. "It tickled my feet just now."

"Hangover's tickling your brain," Bagley scoffed.

Broussard laughed. "Nobody with a brain works for you, mon."

"Mon this," Bagley said, grabbing his crotch with both hands. "Now git, you two. Mother Derringer's oil ain't gonna pump itself."

"Aye, aye, Captain Queeg," Pieton said, clicking his heels like a British field marshal. Bagley smirked, checked his clipboard, and headed for the pumphouse. Pieton jogged toward the derrick crane outlined against the sky like a pearl-handled switchblade. His assignment this morning was to climb to the top and fix the emergency escape system called the Geronimo line.

Broussard watched Pie, his best friend and amigo in the oil

patch, slippery himself up that seven-story ladder like a monkey chasing coconuts. Pie had been a circus acrobat, part of a brother act until a bullet from a Nazi Mauser turned his right foot to corn meal mush. But he still had the moves, and the postwar oil industry, hungry for workers who could ride a typhoon like a carousel pony, didn't care if he limped. He and Pie became fast friends several rigs ago.

"Demmit," Broussard cursed as his toes caught another tremor. This hoodoo was stronger but as quicksilver as the first. He cracked his back and neck bones, hoping to clear the dregs of last night's stew of beer, whisky, and fists. He dropped to the deck and pumped out fifty push-ups, then hopped to his feet for knee bends, jumping jacks, and toe touches. Sweat beaded on his sunburned scalp. *False alarms*, he decided. Those weren't rumbles or mischievous hoodoos, just too many bottles of Jax beer—

Broussard's body whipsawed as the oil rig spasmed like heroin withdrawal. Engineers flew like tenpins. Roughnecks stumbled out of bunkhouse and latrines. Deck planks cracked into jigsaw pieces. Sheet metal howled like a chorus of the dead.

"Blowout!" Broussard shouted over abandon-ship Klaxons as high-pressure methane and crude oil roared from the pumphouse in fine black droplets, each a bomb needing only a spark to explode. "Get to the lifeboats!"

The heaving became an earthquake. A sixteen-year-old assistant cook Broussard admired for his hardworking cheerfulness dashed from the kitchen in a cloud of smoke, his chef whites crackling like fried pork. Broussard tackled him and smothered the flames. "What happened, Cookie?" he said.

"Grease fire," the cook panted. "The first kick upended my bacon fry. That lit up the stove like napalm. Dining room was packed so I fought it till everyone got out." He sucked air as pain waves crashed on his shore. "I ran, but my clothes caught on fire."

"Brave mon, you," Broussard said, checking the young man's arms. The mushroom farm of charred blisters represented second- and third-degree burns. "You'll need doctoring in New Orleans," he said. "Let's find you a lifeboat."

"Can't see to walk, Mr. Remy," the kid said. "I'm half-blind from the smoke."

"No problem." Broussard hoisted Cookie over a shoulder and jogged for the nearest boat. He saw Bagley near the front of the line, knocking one worker after the next to the deck. "Move it, jerkoff, that seat is mine!" Bagley roared. "Out of my goddamn way!"

"Step aside, boss," Broussard said. "This man's bad hurt, he needs to go first."

Bagley whirled. "Did that hoodoo eat your brain?" he snarled. "On no planet does Little Black Sambo take the place of a white man."

"Lucky for him you're not a man," Broussard said, hustling past. Bagley slapped Cookie's face. "Get a rope, Jenkins," he ordered. "I'm gonna string this nig—"

Broussard planted his free hand in Bagley's chest. Bagley flew backwards from the shove, banged off a standpipe, and collapsed like a poleaxed cow. Broussard handed the cook into the boat. Men passed him over their heads and planted him amidships as Broussard squatted at the gunwale. "Get those burns checked as soon as you hit shore," he said. "You don't want them to get infected."

"Why are you giving me a white man's seat?" Cookie said between gasps of pain. "I'm just a poor black nobody—"

"Knock it off. A nobody would have run away, not burned himself saving twenty men from a kitchen fire," Broussard said. He saw crewmen nodding and knew they'd take care of the kid, as they admired courage more than they minded black skin. "I'm repaying our debt with the seat you're in. You have a destiny to fulfill."

"I have a what?" Cookie said.

"A destiny," Broussard said. "That's a dream with a knockout punch 'cause you're going to do it no matter who says no. Your destiny is to do something special with your life." He coughed smoke. "You gave twenty men destinies instead of death today. Now it's your turn."

"I got a destiny," Cookie said, turning the words over in his head. "I got a dream."

"That's right. Now get off this rig and find it."

"Thanks, Mr. Remy," Cookie said. "Thanks a bunch."

"OK, roughnecks, down you go," Broussard said. The tillerman gave him a thumbs up, and Broussard reached for the boat release. Hood-eyed men with ugly expressions crowded him, spewing Bagley's garbage. He folded his arms over his chest.

"I count seven," he said, his voice hard as an anvil. "Get a dozen more you might stand a chance." He cocked his fists. "Cookie's taking this ride no matter what you do. Me, I'd skip your busted noses in favor of hauling ass to those three lifeboats"—he pointed out the half-empties—"and getting off this death trap."

Men looked at each other, at Knockout's ham-hock fists, and bolted. Broussard smiled as they boiled into the boats. *Mission accomplish-mented*, as Pie would say . . .

"You filthy coon lover!" Bagley screamed as he lunged with a knife, eyes bouncing with panic and hate. "Gut you like a fish I will—"

Broussard turned out Bagley's lights with one punch. He snatched the falling blade midair, cut the ropes tethering boat to rig, and slapped Release. The lever was corroded from salt, so he turned around and mule-kicked it. The boat began to lower. He spat at his unconscious boss and started to walk away . . .

Then he turned back and grabbed Bagley's collar. Man had spiders in his head, but he didn't deserve to die in the hell coming. Boots skittering on the oil-slick deck, he dragged Bagley onto another lifeboat and wrestled his dead weight into a seat as workers pushed and shoved for the rest. He sat on Bagley's lap to make room. Bagley groaned. Broussard clonked him in the head with his elbow to keep him from causing further trouble. He bade *Stink Bug* a silent farewell. It would have been fun to test lil' champ under real-world conditions, but he was in a lifeboat leaving momentarily and that was better so—

Pie!

His guts twisted as he jumped to his feet. "Move, move, let me out," he ordered, shouldering through the crowd to sprint across the deck. He'd spotted Pie at the top of the crane, which meant his best friend was stuck. He lost his footing and waterskied his face along the deck, tearing his nose on a broken plank. Ignoring the pain, he scrambled to his feet and got to the ladder. "Why aren't you in the water already, demmit?" he yelled, spitting blood as he climbed. "This rig's gonna burn."

"I busted my pins when the crane kicked," Pieton called down. "Can't get on the ladder or the escape rig. Get you to *Stink Bug*, I take care of myself."

Two broken legs would make that impossible, Broussard knew. He kept climbing as oily smoke balls from the mangled drilling assembly strafed the deck like enemy fighters. Klaxons continued to bray as men who lost the musical chairs for boats held their noses and jumped into the Gulf. *All hands, abandon ship. All hands, abandon ship. All hands . . .*

"We've got to get out of here," Broussard said as he levered himself into the crow's nest. "Blast gonna eat us like grits."

"Trying, mon, but I can't unstick the flywheel." Pieton was propped on one arm, broken legs akimbo, pouring penetrating oil on the Geronimo, the emergency escape system that allowed trapped workers to climb into a steel chair, fly down a sharply angled cable, and cartwheel into the Gulf. "We're going nowhere on this."

"Never did like nowhere," Broussard grunted, inserting a pry bar into a wheel hole and pulling. Pieton upended another can of oil. They felt a pop and the flywheel was loose.

"Take the ride, Knocks," Pieton said as massive I-beams squealed like getaway cars. "I'll arm-shimmy the cable behind you. Done it before in a circus act."

"Even for an acrobat that's too steep," Broussard croaked as smoke wire-brushed his lungs. "Wrap your arms around my neck, we'll Geronimo together—"

A spine-rattling blast pitched them across the crow's nest as a spark lit a cloud of oil and methane. Broussard threw his body over his best friend. Pieton used the momentum to roll them over and plant himself on top. Shrapnel roared through the nest like angry bees. Broussard felt a gusher of warm blood he knew wasn't his, and the weight on his back was gone. He jumped to his feet and scouted frantically for Pie. *Not there . . . not there—*

A fresh gumbo of methane and crude roared out of the well hole a mile below. It rushed past the shattered blowout preventers, up the mile of standpipe that connected oil field to rig, and into the Happy Jack, belching like too much beer. It caught the flames and went supernova. Tons of shredded steel disemboweled riggers and turned unlaunched lifeboats into turkey roasters. It gobbled hammers and wrenches and photographs and ballcaps and coughed them out as charred confetti. Steel beams flew like drinking straw wrappers. Barrels of chemicals arced through the air like poisoned cannonballs. One crashed into the crow's nest. Broussard dove sideways, but a metal edge slashed his head like a broadsword. He faded to black.

Came back.

He blinked a dozen times at the stadium roar in his ears, then frisked himself tip to toe. Nothing broken. One ear was ripped away but he had another. He patted through the blackness for the escape cable. A flying snake of drilling chain wrapped him like a straitjacket and its hot, whippy tail broke his jaw. He spat out broken teeth as he freed his arms from the chain, then searched the crow's nest with fresh urgency. *Not there ... not there ... not there ...*

"Gotcha," he croaked as his trembling hands snagged the cable. The chair was gone, so he yanked off his belt, threw it over the cable, and buckled it. He shoved his arms and shoulders through the loop and braced himself for launch. The sky boiled yellow and sulfurous. He considered the odds of surviving the swarm of steel bees between him and the Gulf. Maybe he could scoot down the ladder instead and launch *Stink Bug.* The curly hairs on his neck started to ignite, and he knew he was out of options.

He whimpered in unaccustomed fear, then reminded himself he was "Knockout" Broussard, father of two and husband of one whom he desperately wanted to see again. His amigo Pie was in the water, ready to make it happen. All he had to do was get there.

He patted the notebook in his pocket, then snugged up his charred dungarees and stared at the burning mosaic that used to be the deck. He yelled "Geronimo!" because everyone liked that on drill days, then launched himself into the smoke. The cable sang sweet as his belt chariot hurtled him toward the saving grace of the Gulf. He let out a war whoop as the shrapnel cloud flayed but didn't kill him.

Then the cable went slack, his forward motion slowed, and he looked up. That last blast had sheared the crane tower from the rig and it was falling his way. He tucked into a cannonball and juked right, saving him from the flyswatter as the crane flew past. He hit the water like a building collapse, but Amélie was fetching the peroxide so he'd be all right. His legs tore off and flew in opposite directions, a symmetry so acrobatic even Pie would be impressed. Water went up his nose and down his throat and he considered for the first time he might be dead, but his arms still worked, so he aimed at the watery sun and swam till he broke the surface. He sobbed in relief as he gulped the salty tang of fresh air.

Then a plunging steel beam broke his heart and dragged him toward the ocean floor and he wanted to hug Lucien and Marcus but the hoodoo in the water said no.

2

... Then a plunging steel beam broke his heart and dragged him toward the ocean floor and he wanted to hug Lucien and Marcus but the hoodoo in the water said—

"No!" Broussard shouted as his brain shook him awake. He struggled to his feet and looked around. He was still in the crow's nest of the derrick crane, so his imagined escape down the cable and into the Gulf was only the dirty trick of the hoodoo. But now what? The blast that knocked him unconscious ripped away the Geronimo. The remaining lifeboats were burning or charred husks. The superstructure and most of the rig had disappeared. His escape pod was surely gone.

He leaned over the rail and was shocked to see *Stink Bug* dangling from its chains, scorched but serene. His body vibrating from fresh adrenaline, he stepped onto the crane ladder and bounced. The ladder was intact, or at least intact enough. He could do this. He was a survivalist down to his DNA. He would survive the hoodoos too.

He began the long, perilous descent. The superheated metal made his palm calluses smoke. When he reached a gap in the rungs, he let go, fell past the gap, and re-grabbed. The jolt from gravity and his weight was brutal, but far less than staying on the crane. A grin split his face when his feet touched the deck.

I'm still here, hoodoo, me.

He stumbled over a shift boss, who screeched in pain then died. Broussard felt the man's spirit soar past him and off the rig forever. He wished the spirit well and stumbled for *Stink Bug*. He was soaked in oil and chemicals, but he was alive, and the notebook was safe inside its rubber and oilskin cocoon.

A violent deck spasm flipped him into a pile of skinless men. He spat in horror and crawled out of their goo. He reached a standpipe and pulled himself back to his feet. A few more steps and he was at the rail.

"Boo-hoo, hoodoo," he taunted as he looked at his escape pod. The bronze glowed blood orange between scorch marks. He spotted the bronze plate his smart-aleck amigo mounted on it several weeks ago. Broussard gave Pie hell about it every day, but he cherished his best friend's engraved gift beyond measure.

USS *Stink Bug*
Constructed by Pieton's unskilled assistant Knockout
Oil Rig Happy Jack
1955 AD

He swung himself over the rail, unlocked the hatch—the combination was Amélie's birthday—and lowered himself inside till he stood on the seat. He was shocked no one had taken his pod. Then again, maybe his reputation scared them from trying, or they couldn't unlock the hatch, or they died before reaching it. Any way you cut it, he was inside the chariot he'd ride to Lucien, Marcus, and Amélie.

He confirmed the floating pontoons were undamaged, then wiggled into the seat and dogged down the hatch, sealing himself inside. He could breathe for two hours before needing fresh air, so he wouldn't turn on the air tank yet. He fastened his seat belt and grabbed the Drop lever, bracing for the violent splash that would come three seconds after disengaging pod from chain—

"Wait, wait," he said, smacking his forehead. He pulled the rubber-wrapped notebook from his pocket and slipped it into the steel box that a decade ago fed ammo belts into the machine guns he'd used to grind Nazis into deadwurst during the Battle of the Bulge. He glanced at his family photos—Amélie and the babies, him and Amélie, the boys and him—then clamped it shut. The gasketed box was so strong and watertight it would survive anything.

"Good to launch, Admiral Knockout," he said. He pulled Drop, yelled "Geronimo!"—because why not—then "Ow!" when he hit the Gulf. He wished Pie was here to see *Stink Bug* swim for real, then break out the cards for a game of hearts.

When he felt himself bobbing gently, he undogged to let in air. It poured through the hatch with a smelly *whoosh*. The escape pod worked precisely as intended. Once he was well clear of the rig, he'd jot a note about its performance under combat conditions.

Another blast erupted from Happy Jack. He peered up to see the derrick crane break away from the rig, just as the hoodoo promised. He hurriedly re-dogged the hatch as seven stories of Indiana steel smashed into the pod. He tumbled like he was inside a washing machine, then came to a sideways stop. Being this far from upright told him the crane had ripped off one or both pontoons. His heart pounded. Without those floats he'd plunge to the bottom, and rescue would be impossible, as even the newest

17

atomic submarine, the USS *Triton*, could dive only seven hundred feet and the bottom of the Gulf was a mile. He began to sink. He clenched his fists, suppressed his welling panic, and vowed to stay alive as long as possible to keep the hoodoo from noticing his boys in the box. He cleared his mind of family, turned the air tank to a slow hiss, and began to sing "Swing Low, Sweet Chariot" in what Amélie had dubbed "Bayou Foghorn."

He sank.

He opened the jar of moonshine he'd liberated from Bagley's locker, gulped half, and smacked his lips.

He sank.

He thought about the Bulge, where he'd killed so many Nazis with determination but no real pleasure, then his wedding night with Amélie, then the birth of the boys, then how he'd taken to bottles and fists and, if he was honest with himself, to roaring drunken fury after Amélie abandoned him for the hoodoo oilman.

He sank.

He munched an apple, drained the bottle, and sang every song he knew as he shivered from the intense cold of ever-deepening ocean.

He sank.

His breathing slowed. His fists uncurled. His eyelids became leaden. He felt as warm as a toasted marshmallow.

He sank.

He watched himself build his cypress house along the bayou and reached up to set a rafter, but the hoodoo said "boo-hoo, you too" and faded his vision to black.

He sank.

3

Present Day
The Azores

Waterlogged hull boards fell left and right, exactly the way Raider planned, creating a "fishing hole" into the room that held the shipwreck's treasure. He briefly savored the tingle that came with every gold rush. Then he used the "fingers" at the end of the submersible's mechanical arms to make the hole big enough to admit his sea drones and other salvage equipment. The submersible bucked. "Steady, Freddie," he said.

"I suggested that to the current," Lime said. "It said bite me."

Raider laughed. A year ago, Lime, his operations guru, stumbled across this fabled shipwreck while testing the AI-powered seafloor-mapping system Raider invented. Research confirmed it was *Las Cinque Chagas*, a Portuguese treasure ship that went to the bottom of the Atlantic in 1594 after English privateers, frustrated they couldn't board after two brutal days of fighting, set it on fire and cheered while it sank.

More important for Raider, the wreck promised fifty million dollars in gold.

After triple-checking the data, he and Lime loaded their support ship with gear, locked their deep-sea submersible *Diver Dan* to its deck, and sailed from Miami to Lisbon to negotiate salvage rights with Portugal. After that came Ponta Delgada, capital of the Azores. The exquisite island archipelago was legally part of Portugal, so Raider didn't need another permission slip, but the Azores were nine hundred miles from Lisbon. Raider knew from a contract he blew early in his career that the longer the apron strings, the fiercer the desire of the locals to show outsiders who was boss—aka, don't treat us like rubes.

The resulting three-way contract ensured that Raider and Lime would handle the recovery and sale of treasure, the Portuguese Navy would shield them from poachers and pirates during the lengthy salvage, and the Azores Maritime Police would ferry out food and tools. Everyone would get rich. It took more time to craft these deals than to scoop up the treasure, Raider swore, but finally, the long-awaited exploration was underway.

As soon as he reinforced the hole from collapsing, his sensor-laden sea drones would find and digitally mark the strongboxes that held their booty. If reality reflected research, this would be their biggest score ever. "Arrrgh, it's a pirate's life for me," Raider murmured.

"What?" Lime said.

"Just daydreaming about our pending riches," Raider said.

"I get that. When I can't sleep, I count gold sheep," Lime said.

"That's pretty good," Raider said. "For, you know, you."

"I'm the heavyweight champion of poets," Lime said. "Like Muhammad Ali."

"What? Ali punched out lights, not sonnets."

"Float like a butterfly, sting like a bee? Is that not great poe-a-tree?"

Raider snickered. "Didn't he also say, Work only gets done if you do it?"

"Naw, you said that, you tyrant." Lime called out topographical dips and rises as he synchronized *Diver Dan* with the currents that swept the sandy ocean floor. This was a shallow-water salvage, but deep was their happy hunting grounds. Thanks to a titanium alloy hull and other exotic engineering, *Dan* was the only treasure-hunting vessel on Earth sturdy enough to reach anything at any depth in any ocean. That gave Lime and Raider a free shot at wrecks everybody wanted but had no way to reach.

To assuage professional jealousy that could bite them in ports, contracts, or sneak attacks on their salvages, they tipped rivals to most of the wrecks they found in shallow waters. It made them a lot of friends, with the bonus that anyone who turned on them was stung by the hive. Crucial calls weren't returned, paperwork disappeared, port officials suddenly demanded inspections, wives were snubbed at parties.

Lime peered through the observation window to check the position of the mechanical arms, then nudged the submersible a degree to port. Iridescent bubbles glowed briefly on the metal skin of the arms, which could deploy any tool needed, from cutter to hammer to wrench. The arms and fingers were so sensitive, Raider could remove a sailor's burst appendix and sew him up in time for happy hour, Lime swore.

A sea creature bumped the window. In the glow of the exterior illumination devices, the creature was a bright reddish orange, with yellow accents and a bell dome that crowned a large, pizza-shaped base. It reminded Lime of the cheesy flying saucers from *Invaders from Mars.*

"Benthocodon," Raider said.

"Gesundheit," Lime replied.

"It's Latin for—"

"A pedunculata, a jellyfish with fine red tentacles in the margin of the bell and yellow gonads which run along its eight radial canals. Yeah, I know."

Raider whistled. "Someone's been reading Wikipedia."

"Only when I tire of Internet porn," Lime said. "Speaking of, am I clear to thrust my steely probe into Mother Earth?"

"Fire when ready."

Lime flipped a switch. A seismographic monitor blasted from the bottom of the submersible and speared the hard-packed sand. They had a contract with NOAA to measure movement in the ocean floor, so they inserted the probe whenever they stopped. Since they didn't have to analyze the data, only collect it, the contract was easy money.

Raider was a whiz at multi-stream revenue. The submersible, support ship, Florida headquarters, and crews for each—not to mention fuel, port fees, bribes to dispense with red tape, and payments to his investors—cost a fortune to maintain. On top of that, for every white whale that yielded millions in gold doubloons, a dozen turned up empty. They never knew what they'd find until their "fingers" did the walking.

4

Isle of Skye, Scotland

"Come along, Gracie," Jennifer Underwood said. "It's time for your treats."

The Highland coo—the gentle, shaggy cow Underwood described to friends as a "musk ox in a mink coat"—turned its curved horns her way and sniffed the air.

"You know I keep treats in the barn, not with me," Underwood said.

The coo looked sad. Underwood laughed. Coos always looked sad.

Gracie followed her to the stone barn overlooking the Inner Seas that formed the eastern shore of Underwood's wildlife sanctuary. She loved Scotland's animals, from eider ducks to whales, pine martens to red deer, ginger-colored coos to the multicolor, maddeningly adorable puffins. Her sanctuary manager did the heavy lifting, leaving her free to talk to Gracie and her "coo-panions" whenever she was here instead of her day job in London. She loved her career and the city, but her heart was in this hilly seaside pastoral she'd resurrected from the bones of a played-out Highlands farming croft—

Shhhhlpppp.

Even if Scotland's eternal rains made her boots stick so hard in the mud that her feet popped out now and then. She looked at Gracie, who appeared to be smiling. "Are you mocking me?" Underwood said.

No answer.

"Well, get in line," she said.

They completed the sloppy trek to the barn where she fed Gracie treats—bundles of the grasses coos ate in the wild but that she'd trimmed to fun-sized—and sea eagles, raptors, and other birds perched on rafter beams during heavy storms. As they became more used to Underwood's presence, heavily antlered deer wandered in and put up with her cooing. Otters and fish splashed in the burns that swept rainwater to the Inner Seas, and the thousands of trees she'd planted when she bought the croft and surrounding land were throwing shade. Not unlike the corporate board of directors for which she worked . . .

"Jen?" her sanctuary manager called through the window. "You have a phone call."

Underwood frowned. "My cell didn't ring."

"Towers are still down from last night's storm," she said. "Charles called the satellite phone at the house. I said you'd call him back, but he insisted I fetch you."

They hopped in the truck and bounced to the croft house Underwood restored from an 1870s ruin to a handsome, sturdy respite from winter wind and summer midges. She'd restacked the whisky-colored stones, installed new walls, floor, and roof, and added a water collection and purification system, composting toilets, electric central heat plus wood-burning stoves, satellite Internet and telephone, insulation, and indoor plumbing. Those were hardly part of the original house design, but her parents' rustic camping adventures across Europe when she was a child were enough "go find a bush, wee lassie, just like our ancestors did" for a lifetime. She strode into the living room and grabbed the handset. "Hi, Charles, it's Jen," she said to her secretary. "What's up?" As she listened, her forehead bunched. "Send the chopper. I'm going back to London."

5

The Azores

Raider groaned as *Diver Dan*'s intercom rang. "How many calls does that make from the poop deck since midnight? Six?"

"Seven," Lime reminded. "The radar glitsch?"

"Oh, right," Raider said, grabbing the headset. "Hey, Phil," he said to the master of his support ship that floated on the Atlantic Ocean and was tethered to the submersible below by cables, hoses, and wires. "Let me guess, the toilets backed up. Wait, really? By when?" They talked another minute, then Raider hung up, shaking his head.

"What?" Lime asked.

"Change in plans. Pull the probe and prepare for ascent."

"We just got here. What happened?"

Raider slapped a bulkhead. "We just won the lottery. But we've got to be in Tangier by midnight to collect."

6

Tangier, Morocco

Raider sipped single-malt whisky as the helicopter grew in the azure sky. He'd hoped to lay over a few days in this mecca of sensual delights—he could wander its spice markets for hours, breathing cinnamon and cracked pepper—but the urgency of their new client's messages suggested otherwise.

"We busted our asses meeting her deadline," Lime groused, draining his umbrella drink while motioning for another. "Then she makes us cool our heels. What a jerk."

"It is what it is."

"Gee, chief," Lime said. "Can I write that down?"

"Shut up and drink your juice box," Raider said.

Lime accepted the fresh glass from the bow-tied waiter. "There's more alcohol in this than your entire bottle of scotch."

"This isn't just scotch," Raider said, popping a slice of truffle-infused lobster into his mouth. It redefined the word *buttery*. "It's a fifty-five Macallan. First release."

"First, ninth, it's all paint stripper to me."

"Said the man with the sippy cup."

Lime smacked his lips. "At least my drink is redolent of Juicy Fruit, Kool-Aid, and Tang. What about yours?"

"Oak and harness leather, with notes of fig, papaya, and pomegranate," Raider said, swirl-coating the Waterford crystal that allowed the Macallan to breathe.

"But is it good or just old?" Lime said.

"Both," Raider said, taking another sip. "Plus it's so expensive it'll remind her we're pay to play. Twenty grand a bottle retail. Triple with the resort markup."

"That's gonna sting," Lime said with a whistle.

Raider tipped his empty glass. The waiter brought another as the chopper roared in for a landing. Titans of industries, militaries, and governments came to this off-the-radar resort to cut secret deals. Elite Moroccan soldiers, knowing who buttered their bread, ensured their privacy. "There she is," he said, nodding toward the helicopter stairs, down which a slender woman with broad shoulders descended. "Miss America."

"Missy swings a meat ax," Lime warned, knowing her reputation as a hard nose.

The woman stopped the waiter, said something they couldn't hear, then glided up, hand extended. "Jennifer Underwood, gentlemen."

"I'm Raider, he's Lime," Raider said. "At your service."

"Even if you're fucking late," Lime said.

A grin creased Underwood's face. "I like a man with bite," she said.

"Saves time," Raider said. "Drink?"

The waiter appeared with two refreshers plus her order.

"Saves time," Underwood said.

They laughed and took their seats. Underwood told her security team to return to the chopper. The lead agent wasn't happy, but he complied. When they were out of earshot, she turned to the table. "Word is, I can trust you both," she said. "Do I have that right?"

"Yes," Raider said.

"Good. Who does what?"

"I'm the show pony," Raider said. "He does all the work."

"Truth," Lime said.

Underwood downed the steaming cup of Kaya Kopi Luwak, the coffee equivalent of the Macallan, and motioned for more. "Sorry to be a party pooper, but I need to wake up," she said. "I've been in too many times zones in too few weeks. If we're destined to meet again, I'd be honored to sip high nectar with men of such sterling reputation."

"Nice of you to say," Raider said.

"Don't let my girlish charm fool you," she said. "I have a serious problem, I need you to fix it, and if you don't, I'll rip off your heads and shit down your necks."

Raider glanced sideways at Lime. "Somali pirates said we'd die that way. When was that, twenty-one?"

"Two," Lime said.

"What happened to them?"

"Smoke on the water."

"Courtesy CIA," Raider said. "We shit too, lady."

Underwood popped a lobster. "Understood, but it wasn't a threat. More to underscore how serious the problem is."

"On a scale of serious," Raider said. "Stubbed toe or broken leg?"

"Ebola," Underwood said.

7

Raider coughed Macallan out his nostrils. "You have our attention," he said, eyes watering at the burn.

Underwood unlocked her briefcase and handed over a seafloor map. "One of our oil wells has sprung a leak," she said. "Gulf of Mexico, Macondo Prospect."

Lime stiffened as if Tasered. "Macondo. That's the Deepwater Horizon."

"Among others, yes."

"But you capped Deepwater," Raider said. "Twice. It's dead."

"It's the Dracula of oil spills," she said.

Lime leapt to his feet, face contorting. "Don't joke about Deepwater, you puke. Do you know how many good people died so you could make a lousy buck? How many kids will get cancer because—"

"Slow your roll, cowboy," Underwood said. "I didn't cause that oil spill and I didn't cause this one. I just have to deal with it." She drank more coffee. "Bang your dick on the table if it makes you feel better, but I'd rather we put that energy into finding a solution, wouldn't you?"

Lime knotted his fists, staring. She stared back, chin up. Finally, he relaxed.

"The dick yields to the sane," he muttered.

She tipped her Royal Albert rose cup at him. "We're not

dealing with the Deepwater Horizon well, thank the oil gods. That cap is holding fine."

"What's leaking, then?" Raider asked.

"Another well in the same Macondo Prospect. It's called Genesis. Are you familiar with under-floor petroleum geography in the Gulf?"

"It's not our sweet spot," Raider admitted. "Treasure hunters work on ocean floors, not underneath. Give us the grade-school version."

She gulped more coffee. "Okay. The word 'prospect' simply means 'an oil field under the floor of the Gulf.' We paid your government for the right to pump crude oil and natural gas from the Macondo Prospect, which is one of eighty-two oil prospects on the American side of the Gulf." She raised a questioning eyebrow.

"So far, so good," Raider said, liking how her delicate brow resembled the side of a violin when lifted.

"Each prospect can hold as many wells as an oil company wants to maintain," she continued. "Macondo has several. Biggest and saddest was the well being drilled by the Deepwater Horizon when it exploded."

"And Genesis?' Lime said.

"It's old, small, and now, leaking. It was drilled by Derringer Oil in the thirties, forties, or fifties—records are unclear. Genesis blew out in 1955, after which Derringer filled and capped it. When we leased Macondo Prospect, we attached monitors to all the wells, Genesis included. The cap is at least seventy years old."

"It was still in good shape?"

"Great shape. That cap was holding up better than caps

half its age," she said. "It passed X-ray and ultrasound tests with flying colors. But given that metal fatigue goes hand in hand with age, we put it next year's replacement schedule." She shook her head. "Man plans, oil gods laugh."

Raider took a sip of Macallan. "Give our hasty summons, you're thinking the failure will become catastrophic."

"Yes."

"How soon?"

She waved off the approaching waiter. "My experts predict the cap will shatter within two weeks."

"Aw, fuck me," Lime groaned.

She looked at him. "Yes. That's why I was late. The engineers grabbed me just before my takeoff from London and gave me that appalling update."

"How much spillage do you anticipate?" Lime asked.

"How many grains of sand on a beach?" Underwood said. "Deepwater Horizon dumped a hundred and thirty-four million gallons of crude oil into the Gulf, plus God knows how much explosive methane."

"Along with eleven rig hands," Lime added.

Her full lips became a thin, compressed line. "I grew up around riggers, Lime. I cried my eyes out when I heard they'd been killed, and that's no fairy tale."

"Makes you a far sight better than your CEO at the time," Lime said. "What was it he whined in that interview? 'I want my life back'? Tell that to the families, pal."

"Most of us at BP were as appalled at his remark as you were," she said.

"That's good to know," Raider said. "But back to the problem."

"Yes. As you know, methane and crude oil are two peas in a pod, always together."

"The dynamite twins," Raider said.

"Atomic in this case. If the cap shatters, the spill will be three times as big as Deepwater, because recent testing shows Macondo Prospect holds a lot more oil than we thought. The more oil, the more gas, the more pressure on the well."

"And its cap," Raider said.

"The weakest link."

"You said three times as big as Deepwater," Lime said. "That means half a billion gallons will pollute the Gulf."

"Not just there," Underwood said. "Currents are heavy right now. Oil will wash up on Mexico's beaches first, then coat the entire Gulf Coast, enter the Gulf Stream in the Atlantic Ocean, and wind up in the United Kingdom. Bad enough we pollute the Americas, but the king will put me in the Tower of London if a drop hits Dover."

"They still chop off heads at the Tower?" Lime asked.

"If that well blows, they'll forge a new axe," Underwood said.

Raider nodded. "What do you need from us, Queen Mary?"

"Speed and precision," she said. "My guys are machining a new cap from a material that will last forever."

"What the last guy said," Lime muttered.

"What I'll say too, and when it fails, so will the next guy," Underwood said.

"BP has capping stacks, right?" Raider said. "You know, well caps attached to an array of rams, blowout preventers, chemical injectors, gas blockers, the whole bit?"

"Gee, no, I've never heard of those things," Underwood said. "What did you call them again, crapping stacks?"

Raider made a face. "Why not attach one to Genesis with a remotely operated submersible? That's how you plugged the Deepwater well."

"Love to, but my capping stacks won't fit. Nobody's will." She waved over the waiter. "All the years I've worked in the business, offshore oil wells have been built to industry spec. That means any stack will fit any well head."

"But . . ."

"Genesis was drilled a century ago," she said. "Offshore drilling was new and wildcat, so everyone sized their wells as they saw fit. This one needs a custom cap."

"Only a cap? What about the rest of the stack?" Raider asked.

"Those take months to manufacture and test," she said. "I have days. My guys can make a simple cap because ExxonMobil found the blueprint of the well."

Lime's eyebrows shot up.

"I know, right?" she said. "It's a miracle. So many records are missing from that era. But ExxonMobil, which absorbed Derringer ages ago, managed to dig it up. My engineers are hot on their lathes. The cap will be ready tomorrow."

"What's our role exactly?" Raider asked.

"BP will fly the cap to New Orleans. A boat will bring it out to you. You'll dive the cap down to the well, remove the cracked one, install the new, and Bob's your uncle."

"Same screw threads? That cap will fit?"

"Yes and yes. I hired those engineers; they'll make it fit, guaranteed." The corners of her mouth twitched. "Even though they nearly got me fired."

"Really? How?" Raider asked.

"Because they existed. I was running BP's engineering shop in 2010. When Deepwater exploded, I hired so many engineers and machinists, it broke my budget. On paper they weren't needed, but given what had just happened, I believed they were mandatory for BP to respond instantly to future spills. Two of my superiors called that an unacceptable waste of corporate funds and plotted my termination."

"Yet here you are, no long knives in your back."

"I had three superiors. My guy's dick was bigger than theirs." She shrugged.

"Let me ask the obvious question," Lime said. "Why us?"

"You're the best. I only hire the best."

"We're the best treasure hunters," Raider said. "Not petroleum engineers. Why not ask Uncle Sam for a nuclear submarine and Navy SEAL divers? With such a serious threat to our national defense, they'd do it for free."

She shook her head. "My prime minister talked to your president. They agree my approach—run silent, run deep—is our best move."

"Points for obscure film reference."

"More points for knowing governments have experts, but you know how to fly under the radar. I need both." Underwood tapped the onyx tabletop, her peach fingernails picking up the tangerine streaks in the stone. "News of this operation cannot leak before that cap is replaced. Can. Not. Sending a nuclear submarine into the Gulf? That hits social media in ten minutes. My PM and your president can't risk the public panicking."

"Neither can your stock price," Lime noted.

She mimicked a cold shudder. "All of which is why I'm in Morocco talking with you instead of in Washington wrestling with bureaucrats, and why I'm going to write you a check so big you can buy a Third World nation. Expertise and discretion."

"Big? You don't know what I'm charging," Raider said.

"If you don't tear me a new one," Underwood said, "I completely misjudged your value."

The security chief trotted up and whispered in Underwood's ear. The CEO blanched. "All right, Sonjay, thanks. Get the chopper ready."

"What's worse than Ebola?" Raider asked.

"Black plague," Underwood said. "My engineers recalculated. Not three times the Deepwater release. Six."

Lime paled. "One billion gallons of crude oil."

"With a *B*," Underwood said. "Methane pressure ramped up too. We now believe a neighboring prospect broke through to Macondo to form one giant pool of hurt."

Raider made a choking sound. "That much methane means we can't use a cutting torch on the broken cap if it sticks during removal," he said. "Even underwater, a spark could blow up half the Gulf. Not to mention blow up—"

"Us," Lime said.

She nodded. "To ensure nothing leaks, I ordered the engineers to lengthen the flange into a skirt, triple its thickness, and add two rows of bolts," she said. "One above the threads, one below, one hundred bolts per row."

"Belt and suspenders," Raider said. "Good. Have your guys bring hydraulic sealant. I'll coat the threads on site and turn that cap into a giant gasket."

"Done," she said, sending off an encrypted text. "If all

that doesn't work?"

"Not our problem. No refunds after the betting windows close," Raider said.

"Which brings us to your fee," Underwood said.

Raider drank Macallan, then held up five fingers.

"That's all?" Underwood raised her eyebrows as she picked up her phone. "Five million I'll wire right now to your bank—"

"Billion," Raider said.

Underwood stared. "With a *B*?"

"Si."

"Jesus Christ, Raider, you want five billion dollars?"

"Lucky for you I don't charge in euros."

"Unacceptable," she said. "For that kind of money, I can buy the Gulf and pave it."

"That would cost ten billion," Lime said. "We're your Black Friday discount."

"One billion," Underwood countered. "I can sell one to my board. Five, they'll keelhaul me."

"Who they gonna call?" Raider said. "*Ghostbusters*?"

"I love that movie," Lime said.

"Aw, fuck me," Underwood said, draining her coffee, then Raider's whisky.

"Work before pleasure," Raider said. "Three."

"One-point-one."

"Seriously?" Raider said.

"All right, all right," she said. "One-point-five."

"Make it an even two. One for Lime, one for me. That's cheap considering you'd spend a hundred billion cleaning up this spill if it happens. Going, going . . ."

Underwood punched her palm twice, then chuffed out a breath. "Deal, you pirates. Now get to work. That well won't unfuck itself."

"I do admire your potty mouth," Lime said.

"You can take the girl out of the oil patch," she said.

"Yeah?" Lime said, perking up. "Which one?"

"North Sea platforms off Scotland," she said. "Da and Mum were petroleum engineers. My sweet sixteen party was under the northern lights at Scapa Flow."

Lime drained his umbrella drink. "All right, Scapa, you walk the walk. We forgive you for being late."

"Thank God," Underwood said. "I would have cried if you didn't like me."

They all started toward her helicopter. The security chief barked orders and the rotors began to turn.

"What was your price before you heard my story?" Underwood said.

"Eight figures," Raider said. "Not ten."

"You screwed me simply because you could?"

"Sums it up," Raider said.

Her face lit up. "If you ever get out of the boat business, give me a call."

Raider's phone rang. He held up one finger and took it. "More bad news, Phil?" he said to his boat master. He listened, and his face crinkled. "Santa Claus is coming to town. Thanks, man, great job."

"Santa?" Lime said.

"Team Phil fixed everything wrong with the boat. We can launch right now."

"Music to the Gulf's ears," Lime said. "I'll head to the

docks. You finish up the 'show me the money' stuff and meet me."

"Roger that."

Lime tipped his cap, then started for the limos the resort used as taxis. Raider leaned against the helicopter's staircase rail. "Sorry for the blowout," he said.

"Gulf or Lime?"

"Same thing. Deepwater bankrupted his brother's fishing business," Raider said, remembering the dreadful phone call from Texas that winter morning. "Lime found him on his boat. He'd blown out his brains with a twelve-gauge."

"Oh, God."

"Yeah. Lime never talks about it, but his anger's radioactive."

Sad lines creased her face. "No apologies necessary. Deepwater was brutal for everyone." She shook her head. "The irony here is that BP is blameless."

"For once."

She ignored the gibe. "Blameless won't matter if there's a spill. We didn't drill the well, we didn't put on the cap. But if oil escapes, we're serial killers."

Raider rubbed his fingers to play the world's tiniest violin.

She rolled her eyes. "Yeah, yeah, whiny CEO. Just get down there and fix this mess, Raider. Everyone says you're the best of the best. Prove it." She knuckle-tapped the helicopter's metal skin. "I'm betting my exceptionally winning career on you."

"And here I thought your concern was for the little fishies of the world."

Underwood snorted. "A ruthless oil baroness who secretly hearts animals. Sounds like the plot of a bad novel." She fished a business card from her purse. "This is my private number," she said. "When you're done saving the world, come visit. You liked that Macallan, right?"

"Who wouldn't?"

"I own a weekend retreat in Scotland. In my library sits an Ardbeg I wouldn't mind sharing with someone who can handle peat and smoke. It's the seventy-two."

"The unicorn?"

She nodded. "The single cask, right."

"Holy grail. I might take you up on that," Raider said.

"Please do. Stay awhile. Scotland's nice this time of year." She let the moment hang a beat longer than necessary. "But first, go do that voodoo you do so well."

"Everyone's a poet," Raider said.

8

Gulf of Mexico

Peering through the submersible's observation port, Raider shook his head at the power of the crude blistering from the crack in the well cap. The plume reminded him of the mighty Saturn rockets that lifted America's astronauts into space, the childhood memory most responsible for driving him to explore his own uncharted territories. The immense water pressure a mile below the surface squeezed the escaping oil into dense blobs, the kind seen in a lava lamp. Each blob wiggled from the power of the current.

"We're gonna need a bigger boat," he said.

Lime nodded. The *Jaws* reference was apropos, because the small leak had grown just in the hours they'd spent prepping the wellhead and both caps. "Surf's up, Mexico to the Carolinas," he said. "If there's a blowout, England will fade to black."

"I saw what you did there," Raider said. "Fade to black? England?" He snapped his fingers. "C'mon, Rolling Stones?"

"Um, yeah, I knew that," Lime said.

"You had no clue," Raider said.

"Hardly a first," Lime said. "How do we slay this dragon?"

Raider considered his options. "Forget finesse," he said. "After removing the broken cap, we'll push the new one into the oil, inch by inch. The stream is weaker than it looks, but that might change, so let's get cracking."

Lime gunned the submersible. Raider confirmed the cap wrench was ready to deploy. Lime told Phil up top they were ready. Underwood, hooked into comms from London, wished them good hunting. Admirals and ministers in Washington and London asked questions. Raider answered, thanked everyone.

"Ready," he said.

"Steady," Lime said.

"Go," they said together.

They moved across the sandy floor like a ten-ton turtle, the mechanical arms swinging the wrench into position as they narrowed the gap to twenty feet. Raider felt unusually heavy vibrations in the hull. "Methane level?" he said.

"Minimal," Lime said after scanning his gauges. "Vibrations are from ocean current, not release of oil and gas."

Raider shrank the gap to ten feet, slipped the wrench over the damaged cap, and selected Counterclockwise. The cap turned like it was greased; those postwar engineers had known their trade. He prayed it didn't stick halfway, as a cutting torch could ignite the methane. He'd have to chisel or vibrate the cap loose, which could warp the wellhead. That would take days to repair, so while hope wasn't a plan, it was all he had.

"Twenty percent unscrewed," Lime said.

"I concur," Raider said.

He'd refreshed his memory during the sail from Morocco. In an oil field, every barrel of crude is accompanied by tons of methane, aka "natural gas." The two were trapped like Siamese twins in the ancient, oil-bearing rocks. When a drill tip punctured the rocks, the naturally pressurized oil and gas moved up the vertical pipe that connected ocean-floor well to oil rig. Devices called blowout preventers kept the black brew on a leash until engineers rechanneled the flow to underwater pipes that fed whichever onshore refinery required a fresh supply.

But if the brew broke the preventers, it charged into the rig unrestrained, creating the feared "blowout." If the blowout hit a flame or spark, it was game over for rig and crew. That's what happened to the Deepwater Horizon on the opposite side of this very oil prospect: methane rushed up the pipe at supersonic speeds, crippled the preventers, swarmed the rig, grabbed a spark, and exploded, creating the shot heard 'round the world.

"Fifty percent unscrewed, everything stable," Raider said as oil streamed from under the cap. "Gas level?"

"Rising but acceptable," Lime said. Ocean water would dilute most of the methane released during their cap swap, but if a gas pocket was dense enough, what happened to the Deepwater could happen to them.

Raider finished unscrewing the broken cap. *One down, one to go.* The power of the totally uncapped stream rocked *Diver Dan.* Lime amped up the stabilizers. Raider tossed the broken cap onto the sandy floor next to the well, then cleaned and polished the threads of the well head. When that was finished, he fished out the replacement cap they'd stored in the cargo bay. He brought the cap to the front of the sub and slipped its outer edge into the whoosh.

"Cap is five percent into the stream," Lime said. "Stable, vertical and horizontal."

"Very good," Raider said. Pushing a blunt object into a powerful stream was not unlike sticking your hand out a car window at ninety mph. If your angle was perfectly flat, your hand knifed effortlessly through the air. Turn your palm a quarter inch and wind pressure kicked your hand like a mule. "Cap is parallel to pipe head. I'm starting the main push into the stream."

"Main push, aye." They held their breath as the eclipse began. "Cap is twenty percent into the stream," Lime said.

"Tell the folks at home," Raider said. BP, Downing Street, and the Oval Office wanted real-time updates. For what they were paying, they'd get their wish.

He read the percentages silently as Lime hurried through the update. *Twenty-five. Thirty. Thirty-five.* Sweat stung his eyes. He ignored it, not daring to release hands from controls. Fifty percent—half in, half out—was the most critical point of this operation because the cap was at its most unstable. The stream could bend it out of true. Break it like a fortune cookie. Tear the arms off the submersible and turn its pilots into fish chow—

Ah-oooga. Ah-oooga.

"Dafuk?" Raider muttered at the digital Klaxon. Methane levels were spiking. He needed to see why, not rely solely on instruments. He re-lit the exterior illuminators he'd shut down to minimize heat and saw a tear-shaped cloud of gas vomit from the pipe. It thumped the bottom of the cap, then squirted sideways, interrupting the ocean current enough to kick-start a vibration that shook the submersible. The vibration turned the mechanical arms into tuning forks, which weakened their hold on the replacement cap . . .

Which popped like a Champagne cork.

Lime let out a string of curses as he switched on trackers. They watched the cap sail over their heads in a lazy, tumbling arc. The methane bubble grew to the size of a cow, undulated briefly, then jumped like a frog. "It's heading for the lights," Raider warned as he lunged for the Off switch . . .

The fireball blinded him through the port. He blinked rapidly to clear his vision. The submersible jinked left, right, left. A moment later it flipped over, crushing them down into their seat belts. Raider felt his tear free. His head smacked the control panel as he fell, and he hit the ceiling-turned-floor unconscious.

"Boss!" Lime shouted. "Are you okay?"

No answer.

"Raider! Wake up!"

He didn't.

"Hang on, buddy, I'll get to you soon as I can." Lime played the controls like a mad pianist, then hopped on the intercom. "A gas pocket exploded, Phil. We're capsized. Raider fell out of his chair and hit his head. He's out cold."

"Jesus," Phil said. "Do you need an emergency ascent?"

"Negative, the well's wide open, I have to cap it," Lime said. "Give me maximum slack on hoses and tethers. I don't want them to tear out."

"Roger that. I asked New Orleans to send a Coast Guard medevac."

"Cancel that, Phil. I need to cap the well before I surface, and I don't know how long that will take. No reason for the chopper boys to waste fuel circling."

"Understood. How about I put in the call again when you leave the bottom?"

"Yeah, that works, thanks, Phil."

"Whatever you need. How's the boss?"

"Breathing appears shallow but steady," Lime said. "He's bleeding from a head wound, but his color is good." He cleared his suddenly clogged throat. "I will not surface until the well is capped, Phil. Repeat, will not."

"I understand, brother," Phil said softly. "Praying he wakes up."

"You and me both—"

"Wait, what? You're not surfacing? What's going on?" Underwood cut in.

"Everything's fine and everyone not Phil stay the fuck off this channel," Lime snarled, choosing aggressiveness to stave off panic among the principals, then clicking out.

"Even . . . me?" Raider groaned.

"Glad you could join the party, Skipper," Lime said, relief flooding him.

"What happened?"

"A gas pillow exploded when it touched the lights. The blast kicked the replacement cap out of the crane arms to parts unknown. Well's uncapped and running free. We're upside down. And you've got a noogie on your noggin."

"Other than that, Mrs. Lincoln, how was the play?" Raider said, struggling to his feet. His legs gave out and he sank back onto the ceiling. "What can I do?"

"Grab that pipe. I'm flipping this tub in three, two, one . . ."

The sub's center jets rolled them right side up. Raider dangled from the pipe a few seconds, then dropped onto a patch of uncluttered floor. That set his head spinning, so he aimed his backside at where he hoped his chair was and fell into it like a sack of potatoes.

"Three-pointer from half court," Lime said. "Now tie yourself down in case we're not done flipping."

Raider grabbed a length of rope from a cabinet and lashed himself to the chair. "Any damage to the sub?"

"Don't think so, but I haven't inspected in detail," Lime said. "I'll do that now if you're okay to drive."

"I've got the helm," Raider said, shaking the wheel to show he had control. "Check for hairline cracks in particular—ayyyyy!" they shouted as oil sneezed from the pipe and sucker-punched the sub.

"Phil to Raider, you're moving awful fast on our trackers."

"A bullet of crude just hit us starboard," Raider said.

"Explosion?" Phil asked.

"Negative, it stayed in bubble form," Raider said. "But it was strong enough to punch us into orbit. Do you have eyes on the sub?"

"Sonar and GPS are tracking you," Phil confirmed. "Good to hear your voice, by the way. If you die, I don't get paid."

"Blackbeard was a sissy compared to you," Raider said, feeling the sub crest the up angle then ride the downward pitch. It landed with a *sssssshhhhh* rather than a thud. "We appear to have landed on sand, Phil, not rocks. Send our map coordinates when you can." He glanced at Lime. "You good?"

"Didn't have time to unbuckle, so I didn't fall."

Raider ran diagnostics and saw green lights across the board. "Submersible appears solid, Phil, and all instruments work." He grabbed a rag from the cabinet and tied it around his head. "Where'd that wallop put us, anyway?" he said, wiping blood from his eyes.

"Far side of the moon," Phil said, sending their location coordinates. "I can't tell you where the well cap wound up, though. The blast fried the cap's embedded GPS, and ship's sonar won't find it; too small."

Raider powered up his AI-based seafloor mapper. It showed scores of metal hotspots, but only one was tiny and perfectly round. "I've got it," he said. "Tell Underwood we're moving to retrieve the cap. Also tell her oil is at full gallop because the well is uncovered, but we'll get that fixed before anyone notices."

"I'll let her know."

Raider started the motors. They hummed like new. "I'll be damned," he said.

"Not till we're done," Lime said. "Are you sure you're up for this?"

"Yeah, yeah. You know how head wounds are, more show than go. The dizziness is gone and you're still a pain in my ass."

"Thank God you're back," Lime said. "I don't like being captain. It's much more fun to complain about all your bad decisions."

Raider marveled at how well Lime performed in a crisis. He'd been trained by the world's leading experts, sure, but this was above and beyond—without his lightning instincts, they'd be in Davy Jones's Locker.

They checked the sub for cracks, leaks, and other damage, found nothing but an oil smear on the observation port. "Run a second diagnostic," Raider said. "If the arms don't work, we'll have to give Jen her money back."

"Yikes," Lime said, punching in the commands. "Green lights, we're gold."

Raider rubbed his head. "Except for my ten rounds with Tyson."

"Two billion buys a lot of aspirin," Lime said. "Speaking of which, why did you tell her you're giving me half? You own the boat, I'm just Gilligan."

"More like Ginger with all your uselessness, but I'll tell you later," Raider said as he plotted their course to the cap. He looked at his watch and decided to update she who paid the bills. "Raider to Underwood."

"Phil told us," Underwood said. "I'm delighted Lime's alive."

"Thanks, Jen," Lime said.

"Hey," Raider complained.

"All right, you too, I guess," Underwood said.

"Nice. I almost died tragically, you know," Raider said.

"Yeah, but you almost made me look bad," Underwood said. "London out."

9

Raider punched in the missing cap's coordinates and juiced the submersible's motors. Lime flipped on the illuminators, which in addition to the white lights that triggered the explosion beamed ultraviolet, X-ray, gamma, infrared, microwave, radio, television, and assorted other waves. Raider's seafloor mapper combined those with the sonar feed to generate real-time composite images that AI refined until they could read labels on bottles. They crept close, closer, closest . . .

"Aw, crap, the cap landed in that graveyard," Lime moaned.

"Of course it did," Raider said. "Given our luck today." He and Lime had run into thousands of such graveyards around the world. People used oceans, seas, lakes, and rivers as trash cans because, out of sight, out of mind. He examined the house-sized shards of metal stabbing the sandy floor. Some resembled salad forks. Others, the charred skyscrapers of 9/11. Pulverized debris created undulating hills of rubble. "Video this for NOAA and the Geological Survey. They'll want to update their maps."

"Roger that. Think this is Deepwater Horizon debris?" Lime said.

Raider shrugged. "We're two miles from the official debris field. This stuff could have drifted here on the currents." He touched his throbbing head. "We didn't survive those blasts to become fish food, so take it slow and easy."

Lime shot him a look. "You're suggesting I drive. Dizziness returned?"

"No," Raider said, gulping Tylenol. "Someone's playing bongos in my head."

Lime took the wheel. "Then sit back and relax, Uber's here."

No response. Lime looked at the skipper. Out again, but gently snoring. Good. Even the toughest bird needed a break.

He sailed cautiously, picking holes and threading needles as they passed dead whales and other animals whose skeletons hadn't yet dissolved. *Oceans are strange brew,* he reflected. Bones in shallow water might stay intact for centuries. Bones in deep water dissolved fast because the harsher water chemistry sucked out the calcium. It's why the families of the eleven missing Deepwater crewmen would never find or bury their loved ones. At four thousand feet below, their bones had disintegrated to powder in mere weeks.

Finally, they reached a metal cage filled with what looked like air tanks—and the shiny oil well cap. "O Captain! My Captain!" Lime sang.

"Uhhhhhhhhgh," Raider said.

"The cap hit that cage at the end of its ride. It broke through the roof and settled on top of those tanks," Lime said.

Raider nodded. "I'll blowtorch the cage and grab the cap. Take ten minutes tops."

"No telling what's in those tanks," Lime objected. "The sub can't handle a third kick in the nuts, so I'd suggest wire cutters."

"I knew I brought a second brain for a reason," Raider said, mentally slapping himself. He knew better than to use a torch, and he never fell asleep on an operation. He might have a concussion or, God forbid, skull fracture.

"Tanks will get loose, you know," Lime said, knowing how much Raider hated adding to trash islands.

"No choice," Raider sighed. "Can't let the shards scrape the cap more than they have, so I have to remove the top of the cage." He powered the snips and began.

"Thar she blows," Lime announced as the first tank floated toward Mexico. Its markings were vaguely familiar, but he had no idea from where or what.

Raider felt a burning annoyance as more joined the great escape. At least they freed the way for him to maneuver. He grasped the replacement well cap and slipped it into the cargo hold. As he finished, one of the tanks, buffeted by a cross-current, bumped across the viewing port. It was eight feet long and two feet wide, with a flat bottom and gently rounded top. What metal wasn't studded with barnacles was a dull olive green. There were stenciled markings—letters mixed with numbers—but they were so faded Raider couldn't make them out. Probably military. Something gassy, he assumed, given the shape. Depleted air tanks. Acetylene for welding. The military industrial complex heaved everything from bullets to baking sheets over the side. "Gee, Admiral, we ran out," was a timeworn excuse to buy more, keep those defense contractors whistling—

Lime inhaled sharply. Raider followed his gaze to the screen. On the ocean floor, beyond the empty cage, a cylindrical object too perfectly formed to be debris glowed dully at the edge of their floodlights.

"The hell is that, a spaceship?" Lime said.

"Klaatu barada nikto, baby," Raider said. "We'll fix the

well, then check it out."

Lime loaded high-resolution images of the new object and the escaped cylinders into the submersible's database. "You OK to drive?"

Raider nodded and gripped the wheel. He picked his way through the rubble as Lime called out obstacles. "Good place for a picnic," he said, shifting to hover.

"Huh?"

"Boss lady gave me something to place on the ocean floor. This is the right spot."

"For what, another oil well?" Lime said.

"O ye of little faith." Raider powered the arms and removed a flat plate of titanium, the only metal that could stand up to saltwater for centuries. He moved it to the front of the submersible. "Train your camera on this and read."

Lime did. "Holy . . . my . . . wow."

"What I said."

"You didn't ask her to do this?"

"Nope. Her idea."

"This is really something," Lime said, eyes welling.

"You gonna cry?" Raider asked.

"Like a baby," Lime said.

"Me too."

"I can't believe her," Lime said. "It's a plaque containing the names of the eleven men killed on the Deepwater Horizon." He refocused the lens. "A photograph of the rig, the date it sank, and 'Rest In Peace.' All engraved."

"She told me to leave it wherever we thought appropriate. She also wants no publicity, nada, zilch. She just thought it was the right thing to do." He tapped his wheel. "Oh, there's one more." He retrieved it from cargo and held it close to the camera.

Lime's bright eyes leaked small streams. "You told her about my brother's death," he murmured. "She made a plaque for him and signed it with love from me and Anna."

"She did, and I think it's perfect," Raider said. "Your brother lost everything when Deepwater bankrupted his fishing business. He killed himself, which became yet another stone for you and your sister to roll uphill."

"That which doesn't kill me makes me stronger," Lime said.

"That shit makes you musclebound," Raider said. "I told Underwood your back story when we were in Morocco, to explain why you lit into her."

Lime's eyes narrowed to slits. "You told her . . . everything?"

"You know me better than that."

"Yeah, yeah, I do," Lime said, waving his hands. "Sorry. It's been a day."

"No worries. We good?"

"As good as it gets for two guys rattled in a dice cup."

Raider laughed. "Underwood felt so bad about his suicide that when she told me about the Deepwater plaque, she asked if you'd be offended if she made this one. She wanted them to go side by side as the honored dead from the Deepwater."

Lime wiped his cheeks. "Offended? Not in this lifetime."

"Make sure the video's running true, then. She should get a copy."

"Damn skippy."

Raider placed the Deepwater plate on the seafloor. Lime

placed his brother's plate and lined it up with the first. They laid rocks around the plates, as if a wreath. Raider said the Seafarers Prayer. "Steer the ship of my life, good Lord, to the quiet harbor, where I can be safe from the storms of sin and conflict. Show me the course I, um, I should . . ."

"The course I should take?" Lime prompted.

"Yeah, but I don't remember the rest," Raider said. "Good enough to count?"

"More than." Lime turned the camera on himself and blew a kiss into the lens. "Thank you, Jennifer. My sister Anna and I will be grateful forever."

"Amen," Raider said. "Let's go cap the well before Mexico needs a dipstick."

They reached the roaring pipe and restarted, ten, twenty, thirty percent. They began to sweat at forty, then pushed though fifty with only the smallest wobble.

"Pressure steady," Lime said. "Methane minimal. Cap seventy percent into stream."

Raider mentally rehearsed what would come next. "When it's directly over the pipe, hold it in place. I'll paint the screw threads with sealant."

"Then we'll lower the cap, screw it down, and tighten the bolts," Lime said. "I read your game plan."

"First time for everything," Raider marveled.

Lime adjusted the sub to the currents as the wrench tightened the cap degree by degree. "When we get home, I'm taking a break from your bossy ass."

"Likewise. Vacation starts right after the next job."

Lime cocked his head. "Next job? What next job? We won the World Series and Super Bowl today, plus you made two billion dollars."

"Of which one is yours."

"And why is that again?"

"Later."

"Fine, be mysterious," Lime said. "Why would you schedule another job before celebrating with her CEO-ness in London? And don't deny you're going, pal. I've seen how she melts your crusty little heart."

Raider jerked his thumb over his shoulder. "Tell you that later too. Because right now our next job is R2-D2."

10

Lime scanned the checklist. "In this galaxy, Captain Solo, the sealant is applied and curing. Flange bolts are in place. Torque wrench is attached to right mechanical arm and ready for your command. May the force be with you."

Raider gunned the trigger that spun the wrench, placed it on the first bolt head, and began. Three hours later, the two hundredth bolt was cinched tight. No methane bubbles. No oil blobs. No explosions. They placed sensors on cap and seafloor and ran three dozen tests. All negative. He yawned and stretched his arms.

"A shame we can't weld," Lime said.

"I do love belt, suspenders, and a diaper," Raider said. "But if we weld, the next crew will have to saw off the cap. Any methane in their water, boom. Best leave this replaceable."

"'Next crew' is right. Every time we poke a hole in the floor down here, the oil gods bite us in the ass. Some crew someday will be back to fix something," Lime said. He cracked a water bottle and drank half. "Shall we go meet R2-D2?"

Raider turned the sub toward the junkyard and made the trek to the wire cage. He demolished it with the arms, then moved to the metal object. Up close, it looked like a sewer pipe with a round hatch poking from the top. Beyond that, they were stumped.

"There's something on the side," Lime said as he peered

through the observation port. "Some sort of plate, engraved. Can you read what it says?"

Raider enlarged the image on the monitor. "USS *Stink Bug*," he said. "Constructed by Pieton's unskilled assistant Knockout. Oil rig Happy Jack. 1955 AD."

"Gee, that clears it up," Lime said.

"See what Google tells us," Raider said.

Lime typed. "Nothing called the *Stink Bug*, whether U.S. or foreign flag," he said. "No reference to a Pieton, whatever that is. Knockout, I won't bother." He typed more. "Hey, an oil rig called Happy Jack blew up in these parts in 1955." He scrolled through the feed, then cursed.

"What?"

"That old well we just capped? It's the one that destroyed Happy Jack with a blowout," Lime said. "Macondo Prospect is a serial killer."

"Why didn't Underwood tell us?" Raider said.

"Probably didn't know," Lime said. "As far as BP and ExxonMobil were concerned, it was a dead well from a century ago. No reason to dig up ancient history."

Raider nodded. "Maybe this thing came off Happy Jack. But what is it?"

"Not just a pipe. Not with that plaque and hatch. Other than that, no idea."

"Well, I declare it buried treasure and therefore belonging to thee and me," Raider said. "It's too big for the cargo hold, though."

"Clamp it in the arms?"

"You read my mind." Raider secured the object and drove toward the coordinates of the support ship as Lime called out obstacles. An hour later, they were directly below. "Phil?" he said. "We're in position and preparing to ascend. Go ahead and call the medevac, then connect us with Underwood and the military."

"Connecting," Phil said.

"Hello from twenty thousand leagues," Raider said.

"If it isn't Charlie the Tuna," Underwood said. "Do you have an update?"

"We are capped and bolted," Raider said. "Six full-spectrum tests over three hours indicate zero gas leakage, zero oil leakage, and zero bubbles. Your well is contained completely, Madame CEO, and the cap your engineers provided fit like the proverbial glove." He and Lime high-fived as cheers erupted from all channels.

"Thank you," Underwood said, her voice husky. "I knew you two would fix this, but hearing the words *zero leakage* . . . well, that's brilliant."

"Wait, you admit I'm brilliant?"

"At this moment, you are. Washington and London have left the air, but I'm quite sure they agree. Come on home, *Diver Dan.*"

"Before we do, Jen, have you ever heard of an oil rig called Happy Jack?"

"Happy Jack," Underwood said. "No. Never. Why?"

"We'll explain topside," Raider said. "Put me back with Phil, will you?"

"Roger that, show pony," Underwood said. "London out."

"Phil, it's Raider. We found an object worth salvaging. Send down a hoist line and cargo net, would you?"

"Roger that," Phil said. "Nice job, you two. Phil out."

Raider slumped in his chair and blew out his breath.

"I'm really glad you woke up," Lime said.

Raider gulped more Tylenol. "Beats the alternative. I'll need a doctor when we get to New Orleans, though. Make sure I don't forget, huh?"

"First I'm your Uber, then your emotional support animal. I'm underpaid." Lime lit an imaginary cigar and blew imaginary smoke into the air. "We're going to get all the love for preventing this disaster, you know," he mused. "The thanks of a grateful nation, medals from Britain and Mexico, maybe a visit to the White House."

"That's bad?" Raider said.

"No, no, it's good," Lime said. "We saved the Gulf from destruction and I'm damn proud we did."

"Then why do you sound like sleet?" Raider asked.

Lime sighed. "Because it wasn't just us. It never is. You and I won the big game. We'll get the Gatorade bath because coach and quarterback always do. But the GM who put the team together? The scouts who argued this guy, not that? Folks who wash the uniforms? They never get jack." He shook his head. "*She* doesn't get jack."

"Underwood," Raider said.

"Underwood," Lime agreed. "Without her, today doesn't happen. Let's make sure she gets a Super Bowl ring too, okay?"

Raider smiled. "Wasn't that long ago you despised her, partner."

"She grew on me."

"Like swamp fungus," Raider said. "We'll make sure she gets that ring. Ship and headquarters gangs too. Without them, we're just two guys telling fart jokes inside a tin can. I'm thinking a million bucks to each person on the payroll. Work for you?"

"One million likes, captain. Now tell me about my money before I get mad."

"Geez, all right," Raider said. "It's simple. You put your ass on the line down here, same as me. You get half the spoils."

"I like spoils as much as the next guy, but a billion is too much. You pay a fortune every year for the submersible, ship, crews, our lab, and investor payments. You take all the risk. I just turn the wrenches." Lime shook his head. "That money is yours, the whole two billion. I appreciate the offer, but I'm happy with just the crew bonus."

Raider shook his head. "You helped save the Gulf of Mexico from total disaster. And you saved my damn life. That means a lot to me."

"Me too. But I'm not stealing half your dough because you got an owie."

Raider thought about it. "How about this, then? I'll take the whole two billion, pay all taxes and expenses, pay off our partners, upgrade everything, and invest the rest. You'll have access to the investment account same as me. Whenever you need money, grab it. I don't care how much you take and you don't need my permission. Just withdraw money."

Lime nodded. "I can live with that."

They shook hands, then Raider popped a bottle of Dom Perignon. "To buried treasure," he said, taking a swig and passing it to Lime. "And saving the world from rot and ruin."

"Hear! Hear!" Lime said. "Nice touch with the Dom."

"They were out of that fruity swill you prefer, so I improvised," Raider said. He drank more and let out a soft burp.

"Underwood said we could open this only if we didn't die or otherwise screw up her bonus."

Lime laughed so hard his nose ran. "She's a good woman, Raider. You have my permission to date."

"Gee, dad, thanks."

"If your wee little scotch bottle hasn't scared her off already, that is . . ."

11

Fort Myers, Florida

Lime punched Play. The "20th Century Fox Fanfare" filled the boat garage as crew members pulled on the prybars Raider carefully inserted under the hatch welded onto the top of the pipe.

It didn't budge.

"Maybe we need a better fanfare," Lime said.

"Yeah, work on that," Raider said. "But meantime, one, two, three, heave—"

"Ho!" everybody yelled as they pulled as hard as they could. No movement.

Raider sighed. "This hatch is dogged down or welded shut. Phil?"

The support ship captain wheeled over a drill as Lime attached the fiber optic cable to his laptop. "From pirates to spy-rates," Raider said as the drill twisted into the pipe. When the bit hit empty space, Phil retracted it and removed the core sample.

"This pipe is marine-grade bronze," he said. "Given its large diameter and thickness, it probably came from a naval vessel. Propeller shaft housing or part of an engine room." He sniffed the black end of the core. "Plain old rubber."

Lime fed the cable through the hole. "We're live," he said as he maneuvered the flexible snake through the interior. "What do you see, skipper?"

"Black rubber covering all interior surfaces," Raider said from the laptop. "At the rear of the vessel is an air tank with military markings. Next to it are a water jug, a bucket with lid, and an ammo can. A few feet forward of those is the back of a seat."

"Single seat? Could this be a one-man escape pod?" Phil said.

"One-woman," Donna Rose, the electrical engineer, said.

"Not in the fifties," Raider said. "They weren't sensitive like us moderns."

"You lugs are sensitive?" Donna Rose said.

"Only at bonus time," Raider said.

Donna Rose grinned. "An excellent point, Oprah. Carry on."

"A million for you, a million for you, a million for you!" everyone chorused.

Raider rolled his eyes. "Watertight escape pods for oil rigs didn't hit the market until the late sixties. Maybe this is a prototype." He examined the seat. "It's metal with military markings. Narrow."

"From a warplane, I'll bet. They were metal because wood was flammable," Lime said. "Fighter plane seats were small enough to fit in cramped spaces, and this is the very definition of cramped." He twisted the directional knob. "What do you see now?"

"The ceiling, also covered with rubber. Toward the bow is the top hatch," Raider said. "There's the wheel to dog it down. That's why we couldn't get in. Submarine-type locking systems are meant to hold back tons of seawater. Makes them hard to breach."

"Military components," Phil said. "Does that tell us anything?"

"Beat up as they are, I'd bet scrap," Raider said. "Military surplus and worn-out parts flooded the market after the war. They'd make for one cheap prototype."

"Solid bronze pipe," Phil said. "Whose welds are perfect, which is difficult to do on bronze. This pod didn't crush or leak for seven decades. Whoever made this knew his way around a tool belt." He heard Raider clear his throat. "What, skipper?"

"We have a body," Raider said. "More precisely, a skeleton, strapped into the front seat."

"Maybe our builder," Lime said. "What else do you see?"

"An empty bottle of booze."

"Good for him," Donna Rose said.

"Had a sense of humor too—the label says Olde Homicide." Raider stood up. "Check the video, see if we captured everything, 'K?"

Lime sat at the laptop. "We did, bow to stern."

"All right, pirates, because of the skeleton, I'm declaring this vessel a burial site," Raider said. "We'll leave it alone till somebody smart figures out who's inside."

The crew bumped fists and began to clean up.

"I've seen my share of bodies," Lime said. "But never one locked in a pipe. Who do we call about that?"

Raider considered the options. "State and federal forensics labs will take a year to get to this, backed up as they are with crimes. Let's send the pod to our private lab."

"Only the best for Skelly," Lime said. "Do we FedEx it, or what?"

"We'll deliver it ourselves," Raider said. "Lab will obtain DNA samples via the hole we drilled. If they find a match from any DNA database, they'll notify next of kin. If the kin want the bones and this pipe, the lab will remove and pack the bones and deliver both. If the kin decline or none are found . . ."

"Back to the sea," Phil said.

"Works for me," Lime agreed.

12

Six Months Later
Interstate 10

"Driving Miss Raider is such a burden," Lime said from the driver's seat of the limousine. "How do you put up with him?"

"He grew on me," Underwood said from the back, threading her arm through Raider's.

"Like swamp fungus," Raider said, interlacing his fingers into hers. "Jeeves, we've been on the road two hours, and that only after flying from Fort Myers to New Orleans. Where the hell are you taking us? Pluto?"

"All will become clear in the fullness of time," Lime said.

"You keep saying that, but we never get there," Raider said. "You're so mysterious now that you have money."

Lime leaned into the southbound turnoff. "You know, Jen accepts my gifts with graciousness. Be like Jen."

"I should have left you at the bottom of the Gulf," Raider said.

"You almost left yourself, that hit on the head you got. Is it true the surgeon filled the divot with skin from your gluteus maximus, making you a literal butthead—"

"Enough, you two," Underwood said. "I think it's sweet he arranged this surprise for us."

"He kept it secret, though," Raider said. "I hate secrets."

"Do you always have to be in charge?" Lime asked.

"How long have you known me? Of course I do."

"Tough. This time, I'm lead dog and you're sniffing my hairy—c'mon, Jen, help me out. Give him counsel or hit him with a tire iron or something."

The CEO of BP grabbed Raider's shaggy curls with both hands. "Sweet silence," Lime sighed as they kissed. "Wish I'd suggested that ages ago."

"Me too," Raider panted. "But we only met the lady six months ago."

"Met her money too," Lime said, waggling his eyebrows in the rearview. "Jen, you really should dump Raider and hang out with me. Why let that loser drag you into the mud when you can be with the man who saved the world?"

"Oh, honey, you know I would," Underwood cooed, batting her eyelashes. "But you don't need my help. You're already so handsome and accomplished."

"That's true," Lime said. "Also, brainy—"

"Are. We. There. Yet?" Raider groaned.

They laughed.

"This seems like a good time to tell you both," Underwood said.

"What's that?" Lime said.

"The board nearly fired me over how I handled this."

Raider stiffened. "Why? You saved them from an oil spill and bankruptcy."

"They like that part," Underwood said. "What they didn't like was not telling them ahead of time."

"You couldn't," Raider said. "Your prime minister swore you to secrecy."

"I know that. You know that. They even know that. But they think they're entitled," she said. "Which they are, I suppose. I serve at the pleasure of the board." She made a strangling noise. "Not telling them was the third strike. First was, I paid you two billion dollars without asking please. Second was that bacchanal you threw."

"That was an epic party," Lime said fondly. "I think everyone in Fort Myers stripped naked, got drunk, and lit their cigars with our hundred-dollar bills."

"Best party I didn't dare attend," she agreed. "But it hit social media and my directors saw it. They didn't see the, um, humor."

"Puritanism is the haunting fear that someone, somewhere, might be happy," Raider said.

"H.L. Mencken's best line," Underwood said. "But the board expects me to run major decisions past them before I execute, and I didn't."

"You had good reason," Raider said.

"Reason has nothing to do with it," she said. "This is power, red in tooth and claw."

"Fuck those guys," Raider said, his never completely buried anger at BP starting to bubble. "Why didn't you tell me you were in trouble?"

"I carry my own burdens, Raider."

"But I could have done something."

"Like . . ."

"Geez, I don't know. Sent exploding cigars to the board?"

"They would have blowed up real good," Lime said.

Underwood laughed at the homage to SCTV. "You're right, Raider, I should have told you sooner. I get too protective of my independence for my own good."

"Pot talking to kettle," he said, kissing her cheek. "In your defense, we've been crazy busy, so let's agree it slipped your mind."

Underwood sighed. "Crazy busy is right. You went on your own press tour, then repaired the submersible. I ran a million BP strategy sessions, then the international press tour, *then* a task force to update blowout preventer systems. In between I did some, you know, actual business."

"Oil exploration?" Lime said.

"Bacteria."

"Bacteria? The little critters that make us sick?" Raider asked.

"Their cousins, who turn garbage into fuel," she said. "World's changing, gents. We change too or get left behind." She looked at Raider. "The few times we squeezed out a couple days together, the last thing I wanted to do was talk business."

Raider tented his fingers and bowed slightly.

"Third strike normally means batter out," Lime said. "Yet this morning's *Times* quoted you as CEO of BP."

"I'm still employed."

"For how long?"

"Unclear," she said. "In my favor, you two saved the world from a disaster that would have bankrupted BP. The thanks my directors received from every head of state gave them the warm and fuzzies. The prime minister confirmed to the chairman of the board he'd ordered me to not tell anyone on grounds of national security."

"Doubling the stock price in six months didn't hurt," Lime added.

"'Show me the money' is next to godliness in business," Underwood said. "Hey, no complaints. I wanted CEO, and getting fired is part of the risk. I wouldn't change a thing, including your party. Throw me one of those when I retire." She set her jaw. "Underline retire. They fire me, I'll shove it up their ass. Nobody puts Baby in a corner."

"What would you do if they did, though?" Lime said. "Knit booties?"

"God, no. I stab my fingers every time I knit," she said. "Maybe I'd form a hedge fund, take over BP, and make the board assistant gas station managers." Her smile radiated mischief. "Or open a wildlife sanctuary to take care of the little fishies of the world."

Lime snorted. "Yeah, right. The Joker would marry Batman before an oil baroness hearted an itty-bitty fish."

Raider suppressed a laugh. Jen's Scottish mud had sucked his feet out of his boots more than once, so he knew her secret heart. "I predict our gal will keep making the doughnuts for Mother Beep," he said. "But to pad her resume just in case, she can take your place on the sub."

"You'd fire me?" Lime said. "After I saved Jen's bonus?"

"You'd fire him?" Underwood said. "After he saved my bonus?"

"Gilligan's taking a vacation," Raider said. "I need to get back to the Azores before someone jumps our treasure ship claim. And you need to see a pedunculata."

"A what-culata?" Underwood said.

"Sea creature with yellow gonads," Lime said. "Like Raider."

Underwood burst out laughing. "All right, I'll take a ride

in your tin can. But I won't wear a little white sailor suit."

"Spoilsport," Raider said.

The SUV darkened as rear window shades moved into place.

"Excuse me, Jeeves," Raider said. "We're too old to do it in the back seat."

"Speak for yourself," Underwood said.

"You're young at heart and limber of spine. Me, not so much."

"You'll do," she said. "But why are the shades closed, Harry?"

"Because we're only five minutes away," Lime said.

"From?" Raider said.

"Home."

13

Thibodaux, Louisiana

Lime opened the passenger door. Underwood stepped onto a gravel driveway, followed by Raider. They blinked at the welding-torch sun, which was hazy with bayou humidity. Raider kicked a stone toward a low, sturdy house crafted from a reddish-brown wood he couldn't identify. It bounced off the stairs of a wraparound porch made of the same wood. A muddy waterway to the right of the house meandered through mangrove islands as far as the eye could see. The smell of grilled food danced through the air.

"What is this?" Raider said. "Cajun Oz?"

A woman stepped from the inky shade of the porch. Her smile was warm and her bearing confident. Her olive skin was accented by dark brown hair and eyes. Dust devils spun from her heels as she walked their way.

"Welcome to the bayou," she said. "I'm Catherine Broussard."

"I'm Raider," he said, offering his hand. "This is Jennifer Underwood. I understand you already know Poop Deck Lime."

"I do." Catherine shook hands all around. "I'm delighted to meet the rest of you. My father is too. He's waiting for you out back."

"Where all will become clear in the fullness of time," Lime said.

"Clear," Raider said, rolling his eyes. "You keep using that word. I do not think it means what you think it means."

"Inigo, buddy, just go with the flow and you'll win the princess bride."

Catherine laughed. "This is normal for these two, I gather?"

"I'm afraid so," Underwood said. "But give them time, they grow on you." She breathed deep. "Is your father responsible for that delicious aroma?"

"Dad's quite the cook, so yes. Please follow me."

They walked along the burbling water to the back of the house and stepped onto a riverbank alive with wildflowers and cypress. A trim, older man in jeans and untucked linen shirt was placing food onto grills built from metal drums. He reached into a cooler, retrieved a bottle of lemonade, and drank half in a single swallow. He put it on a tree stump, then employed a squirt bottle to douse flare-ups licking the food.

"I hope you came hungry," the man said.

"No problem there, sir," Raider said. "But who are you?"

"Lime said you'd ask," the man said. "He said the answer is . . ."

"All will become clear in the fullness of time," everybody chorused.

"Very good," Lime said.

"I'm going to humor you, pal," Raider said. "Until the moment I strangle you."

"Please don't kill him before lunch," the man said. "Without Mr. Lime, I'll have made too much food."

"No such thing as too much food," Raider said.

The man laughed. "You're my kindred spirit, you." He

piled platters high with seafood, meat, and vegetables. He set them on a long table made from planks the same color as the house, walked back to the grill, and returned with an iron pot of gumbo that steamed like a Civil War locomotive. He ladled the thick stew into bowls, put one at each place on the table, and wiped his hands on the towel hanging from his belt. *Lolo Café: Great Dining, No Whining* was embroidered in red, white, and blue in the center.

"My name is Broussard," he said, shaking hands all around. "Call me Lucien. Catherine is my daughter. We invited you today to help us celebrate."

"Celebrate?" Raider asked. "Celebrate what?"

"A knockout," Lucien said.

14

Raider and Underwood looked at each other. Catherine held out a platter. "We'll explain, we promise," she said. "But first try this. It's dad's favorite. I think you'll like it."

Raider popped the coffee-encrusted pork loin into his mouth. It was better than the truffle lobster back in Morocco. "It's excellent," he said, licking his fingers.

"Thanks," Lucien said. "The gumbo should be cool enough to eat without burning your mouths, so please take a seat."

They settled onto the long benches that flanked the table. "You're clearly nice people," Raider said. "But I'd enjoy lunch more if I knew why we were here."

Lime raised his beer to Lucien. "I think we've kept them waiting long enough."

"I agree, it's time." Lucien stood and cleared his throat. "The skeleton you found in the Gulf of Mexico is my father," he said. "His name is Remy Broussard, but everyone called him Knockout. You treated him with respect and you brought him home. We appreciate it to the bottom of our hearts."

15

The stunned silence was broken by a loud, slapping splash near the water's edge. Underwood jerked in her seat. "What was that?" she said.

"Alligator," Lucien said.

"I need another drink," Underwood said.

Lucien laughed and poured her lemonade with three fingers of vodka. "How much of the story do you know?" he asked.

"Some," she said. "But certainly not all. Begin from the beginning."

Lucien nodded. "While replacing the cap on your well, Raider and Lime ran into a bronze container of unknown origin on the floor of the Gulf. They claimed it as buried treasure, but when they examined the interior with a fiber-optic camera, they found a skeleton strapped into the pilot's seat. They stopped the examination and turned everything over to a DNA lab for analysis. Lab tests proved the man was my father, Remy Broussard."

"Why did they call him Knockout?" Underwood asked.

"Because he was a fighter, in every sense of the word," Catherine said. "Size, strength, loyalty, heart, attitude. My grandfather could hardly read or write English, preferring Cajun French instead, but he had a deep understanding of people. He loved to fight, loved his wife and sons, and loved the oil business, in that order."

"He worked on the Happy Jack?" Raider asked.

Lucien nodded. "He operated the derrick crane. When a blowout destroyed the Happy Jack in 1955, it went to the bottom of the Gulf, and so did he."

Underwood put her hand to her mouth. "I'm sorry. What a terrible way to go."

"Thank you," Lucien said. "My father's spirits were alone in the dark all those years. You brought him into the light." He pointed at the house. "Dad built this as a wedding gift to my mother, Amélie. She's dead, as is my brother, Marcus. I live here still."

"You always will," Catherine said.

Lucien squeezed her hand. "I hope so. I'd like to finish my life where it began."

"I don't blame you," Raider said. "This architecture is stunning, all the grain and texture of the wood. It looks like it can ride out any hurricane."

Lucien nodded. "My father built it from solid cypress he felled on this very property." He pointed at the stump holding the squirt bottle. "Cypress is rotproof and stronger than a gator's jaw. Perfect for the bayou." He poured himself more lemonade. "The state declared him dead after the blowout. The preacher held a service, which was nice, but I'd always wanted to bury him physically." Sadness washed his sun-bitten face, then disappeared. "Thanks to you, we can."

Underwood hugged Catherine. "The boys found your long-lost family."

"You did too, Ms. Underwood," Lucien said. "Mr. Lime explained your crucial role in this saga. If it weren't for you and them, we'd have gone to our own graves not knowing about his. You're as much la meilleure as they."

"That's nice of you to say," she said. "But what is a la meilleure?"

"It's Cajun French," Catherine said. "In translation it means 'the best one.' It's my father's term for people so exceptional, he puts them into the pantheon of the gods."

"Me, a god," Raider said, thumping his chest. "Whoda thunk it?"

"Nobody," Lime said.

Everybody laughed. "I've been many things in my life," Underwood said. "But never la meilleure. Thank you, Lucien."

Raider cleaned his gumbo bowl. "The moment we saw the bones, I shut down the project," he said. "Not all treasure hunters honor the sanctity of burial sites, but we think it's right." He looked at Lime. "How did you know all this and I didn't?"

Lime ate some coffee pork and blew a chef's kiss. "Timing. After the lab identified the remains and informed us the family wanted them, you flew off to London, happy they'd be reunited but happier to hang out with Jen. Two days later, Lucien called our office in Fort Myers. He said he wanted to thank us in person for recovering his father. I explained how insane our schedule was then, and suggested I bring you and Jen for a visit when it eased up. Lucien proposed I make it a surprise."

"And here you are," Catherine said. "Surprise."

Lucien leaned on both elbows, wonder on his face. "The odds today would happen were a billion to one."

"Trillion," Catherine said.

Lucien nodded. "First, my father had to build an escape pod, as none existed commercially in 1955. Second, he had to get himself inside when all hell was breaking loose. Third, the pod could not be crushed by water pressure."

"Fourth," Catherine picked up, "Raider and Lime had to find a needle in a haystack. The Gulf of Mexico is the world's largest ocean gulf."

Raider swirled his beer. "Fifth, he had to have known to choose bronze because steel would have rusted out. The man's welds and hatch seals were perfect, so *Stink Bug* stayed intact and watertight for seventy years."

Lime raised six fingers. "Which prevented saltwater from getting into the pod," he said. "Which kept his bones from dissolving, which allowed the lab to collect his DNA and identify him."

"How did the lab match the DNA to Remy specifically?" Underwood asked.

"Several years ago, Catherine asked me to register him in the national database of missing persons," Lucien said. "I had some of my father's keepsakes and brought them to the office in New Orleans. They extracted his DNA from roots they found in his hairbrush. I never expected it to come to anything." He ate some gumbo. "They got a match from the skeleton and called me. I asked who'd found him. They said they couldn't tell me for privacy reasons, just like they couldn't tell you about us." He grinned. "But I got a warrant."

"Dad's a game warden," Catherine said. "Louisiana Wildlife and Fisheries. He's the best in the business."

"Aw, hell, girl, I just write fishing tickets," Lucien scoffed.

Lime sensed Lucien did far more than that. "Some fish are bigger than others, though, right?" he said.

Lucien smiled. "Surprising how big some grow. Anyway, I

served the warrant, and they provided your contact information. I called your shop in Fort Myers—Burnt Store Road is quite the Dickensian street address, by the way—and Mr. Lime answered."

"Lucien and I talked, then I hopped in the car and drove down here," Lime said. "I told them how we'd found the pod and bones, and they cooked up this surprise."

"Literally," Underwood said, dipping gator into gumbo.

"It seemed a fitting way to end our adventure, sharing a meal with Knockout and his family," Lime said. "I rented the jet and limo and told Raider and Jen to clear their calendars."

Raider's eyes brightened.

"I had plenty of allergies too when the DNA lab called me," Lucien said, patting Raider's shoulder.

"What else can you tell us about your father?" Underwood asked.

Lucien stood and cracked his back. "He was a rough-and-tumble Cajun who wrestled alligators for spare change, loved bar fights that turned into brawls when the deputies arrived, and enjoyed life on the oil rigs," he said. "By all accounts he adored my mother, Amélie, my brother, Marcus, and me."

"Do you remember him?" Underwood asked.

"Very clearly, but not completely," Lucien said. "He died too young for me to get to know the man in full. From everything I can tell, his love for us was genuine, even if he wasn't home much because he needed to put food on the table. Part of him was a decent and honorable man and father."

"The other part?" Raider said.

"Volcanic. Amélie wanted a more exciting life than bayou housewife, and she got it by abandoning us. But before she left, her many infidelities put spiders in my father's soul. Her walking away for good turned him into an alcoholic, rage-filled brute." He smiled without humor. "Life in our home wasn't *Leave It to Beaver*."

"I hear ya," Lime muttered. "Did your mother collect you after he died?"

Lucien smiled without humor. "We never saw or heard from Amélie again, despite both of us writing letters to her last known address in Houston. Then my brother died of cancer, and I was on my own. It wasn't until years later I learned she'd been murdered in Houston. It wasn't about her. It was a message to her husband, who kept failing to pay back the mob loan he'd taken to expand his oil business."

Underwood clapped her hands to her face. "Lucien, I'm so sorry. Did the police find her killers?"

"Police didn't bother because they were mobbed up too," Lucien said. "But a friend of mine tracked down her killers. They paid in, um, full."

"How did your friend—"

"Let's not talk about all that, Jen. Today is about my father, and you."

Underwood squeezed his hand. "As you wish, Lucien. What do you know about the Happy Jack explosion?"

"Almost nothing. At the end, Remy was practically alone when the rig exploded. The rest of the crew was either dead or had abandoned ship." His voice misted just a bit. "Pie was part of the former, God rest his soul."

"Reville Pieton," Raider explained. "His name was on the plaque. 'Constructed by Pieton's unskilled assistant Knockout.'"

"Pie was my father's best friend," Lucien said. "They

ribbed each other mercilessly as a show of affection, as men did then. He talks a lot about Pie in the notebook."

"Notebook?" Raider said.

16

Lucien smiled, this time with warmth. "Did you see that ammo box?"

"I did, during our video search of the pod," Raider said. "But we didn't examine the contents because we didn't open the pod."

"Inside that box was a notebook my father kept for us boys," Lucien said. "He was away from home for months at a time, so he thought we'd enjoy reading about his life on the oil rigs. He stored the notebook in that box when it wasn't in the pocket he'd sewed inside his work shirt. During down times, he'd write a few sentences to me and Marcus."

"He wrote notes to his boys. I love that," Underwood said, resting her chin on her index finger. "What did he talk about?"

"Himself. Pie. Boss Bagley. Amélie. Us boys. Whales, how constellations changed with the seasons, weather reports, which were always a variation of 'I know you won't believe this, boys, but it's hot and humid today!'"

Underwood fanned herself. "Hot and humid in the south?"

"Hard to believe, I know," Catherine said. "What else did he write about, dad?"

"Day-to-day life on the rigs. His idea for a one-person escape pod, the drawings and specs for which are in the back of the notebook. Eisenhower-era politics. How Amélie was coming home any minute. That last was a constant drumbeat."

"He really believed she would, didn't he?" Lime said.

"With all his heart. He believed it was their destiny to reunite and we'd all be happy again," Lucien said. "In that sense, my father was a hopeless romantic." He made a gesture with his shoulders. "His escape pod was remarkable."

"I'm all ears," Raider said.

"After the war, tons of worn-out ships, tanks, planes, and other military equipment were loaded onto garbage scows and dumped in the Gulf," Catherine said. "My grandfather found what he needed and made the rig with his own two hands."

Raider raised an eyebrow. "All by his lonesome? Serious props to his talent."

"Grandpa could make any tool sing," Catherine said. "He built this house from cypress, he crafted that pod from bronze."

"Sounds like you know a lot about him," Lime said.

"Between dad's memories and the notebook, yes," she said.

"I just wish I knew about his final hours on the rig," Lucien said. "His last entry was how his boss made him climb a stinky rope to get to the working deck. Nothing about the blowout or explosion."

"I work in the oil patch, Lucien," Underwood said. "I can get any records that still exist. Who owned Happy Jack?"

"Derringer Oil and Refining Company of Texas," Lucien said. "Which was bought by Standard Oil of New Jersey, aka Jersey Standard, which renamed itself Exxon, which merged with Mobil, aka Standard Oil of New York, aka Socony-Vacuum Oil, and renamed itself ExxonMobil. I appreciate your offer, Jennifer, but I've asked. That friend I mentioned, Parson

Dumont, is a private investigator. He says all reports of the blast were lost in transit from one corporate headquarters to the next."

"More likely the files 'disappeared,'" Underwood said, adding air quotes. "Paper records were easy to tragically misplace when explosions needed whitewashing."

"I don't doubt it," Lucien said. "He lived, he loved, he worked, he died. That's the sum total of my father, Remy Broussard, may he rest in peace."

Lime grinned at Raider. "See?" he said. "It all became clear in the fullness of time."

"I won't give you the satisfaction of agreeing," Raider said.

"That satisfies me even more," Lime said as everybody laughed.

"How was his funeral service, Lucien?" Raider asked. "Did it give you any peace?"

"It will," Lucien said.

"Will? Present tense?"

"Technically, future tense," Lucien said. "But present tense works—"

Raider jumped as "When The Saints Come Marching In" blared from the side of the house. A funeral jazz band appeared, a dozen men and women high-stepping the riverbank in black uniforms and coats. "Swamp Steppers" was embroidered in gold on their shiny billed hats, and trumpets and trombones gleamed brassy in the sun.

"Come on, everyone, we're going to bury my father New Orleans style," Lucien said, hopping to his feet and swaying to the music.

"Folks here like a little funeral with our music," Catherine said.

Lime felt his phone vibrate. He checked it, then stood. "Hang on, everyone, please listen to me!" he shouted. "It's important you know this before the funeral begins."

Lucien motioned for the band to take five. Musicians ambled to the waterway to smoke. "The floor is yours, sir," he said. "Though I know not why."

"I apologize for stepping on the funeral, Lucien," Lime said. "I promise we'll get back to it as quickly as possible. But I arranged a surprise for your family, just like you arranged this surprise for mine."

"A surprise?" Lucien said.

"We're family?" Raider said.

Lime punched Raider's shoulder. "Yeah. You're the idiot brother."

Lucien nibbled a lobster tail. "Isn't that lovely, a surprise for us. Well, Knockout has waited this long. He'll happily wait for your fullness of time."

"I promise you won't regret it," Lime said as a black limousine appeared at the foot of the driveway. Lime hurried over and opened the door. A slender, elderly man climbed out of the back and looked around. Lime shook his hand, spoke briefly, and offered his arm. The man took it. When he reached the riverbank, he let go and slowly walked toward the table, his back heavily bowed but his bearing dignified.

"Everyone, meet Codell Smith," Lime said. "Codell, meet Raider, Jennifer Underwood, Catherine Broussard, and her father, Lucien Broussard."

"A pleasure to know you, Mr. Smith," Lucien said. "Would

you like something to drink or eat? I made plenty."

"That would be most pleasant," Smith said, stroking his neat, pointed goatee. "If it's not too much trouble."

"No trouble at all," Catherine said, motioning him to the table. He didn't move. "Mr. Smith, please join us."

"Call me Codell, and yes, I will," Smith said. "But I need to tell you something while I'm standing."

"Is it more important than gumbo and lobster tail?" Lucien asked.

"Yes, sir, it is."

"Then you surely need to tell it," Lucien said.

Smith stood until his back was straight.

"The day I caught fire," he said, "your father saved my life. Remy Broussard is the finest man I'll ever know, and I'm here to tell you why."

17

Lucien's eyes widened. "You knew my father? On the Happy Jack?"

"I'm proud to say I did," Smith said. "You, Marcus, and Amélie too, in a way. He told me about his family on the nights we shared cigarettes on the Happy Jack. I was with him the day of the disaster. That I survived was due entirely to his morality and courage."

Lucien sagged. "Please sit down, Codell," he said. "I know I need to."

Catherine told the band there'd be a delay, then joined the table. Smith accepted a bowl of gumbo and lemonade with vodka. Lime mixed himself the same drink.

"I was a cook on that rig," Smith said. "A skinny black teenager in the hard white world of Louisiana oil. Your father was a senior member of the crew."

"Remy was a crane operator, from what I understand?" Raider said.

"More than that," Smith said. "He was an oil whisperer, a true god of the oil patch. The company liked him, the crew adored him—his strength carried us all. Some nights he couldn't sleep, so he wandered out to the deck rail to look at the stars. If I was there on a break from night kitchen, he shared his cigarettes with me. Other black men too. We blew smoke rings, told stories, shared laughs. Us, Remy, and whoever would join along."

"You smoked with white men, Codell?" Lucien said, raising an eyebrow. "And lived to tell the tale?"

Smith's brown eyes glittered. "Most of the crew were war veterans. They respected each other's service even if their skin was different. And truth be told, most of the old boys were harmless enough. 'Hey, Knocks, why you hanging with them boys, ain't your skin dark enough already?'"

Lucien looked amused. "They call us Cajuns white folks, but our skin comes in all shades. My father's was French roast. I got lightly toasted. Codell, please go on."

"Remy would say, Come on over, boys, smokes are on me," Smith said. "Many declined, but some came to the rail. We smoked together, peaceful-like, just looking at the ocean and stars." Smith's expression darkened. "That said, we did have a few Klanners on board. One said to my face he'd rather string me up. Remy told him I was good enough to cook white eggs, so I was good enough to smoke white cigarettes, and if the man had a problem with that, Remy would shove his lynch rope up his ass and floss his teeth with it." The darkness dissipated. "Your daddy was Hercules, Lucien, no fooling."

"Were you with him the day he died?" Catherine asked.

Smith pulled up his sleeves. The scars were thick and ropy, like tree bark with beetle holes. "Yes, ma'am. Nearly up to the end."

"Are those from the blast?" Lime asked, suppressing a shiver. His father had burned such scars onto his back when he was eight for the "crime" of talking back . . .

"Indirectly," Smith said. "The first burp from the well didn't ignite, but it rocked the rig so hard, a pan of bacon flipped over on the stove. That started a grease fire. I fought it till everyone evacuated, then ran. But my uniform was covered with grease and went up like a rocket." He winced, remembering. "Your father threw me down on the deck and smothered the flames. That was second of the three times he saved my life."

"What was the first time, Codell?" Underwood asked.

Smith accepted a drink refill. "When a welder claimed I'd screwed up his breakfast order."

"Did you?" Raider asked.

"No. I cooked his eggs sunny side up, exactly how he ordered. But no way I could contradict him, not in 1955. Instead, I apologized and said I'd remake his plate. He slapped me so hard I saw stars. Then he grabbed my collar and drew back his fist."

"Whatever for?" Lucien said.

"Because he could. Man just found out his girl was fooling around back home, so naturally, Sambo had to pay." His smile was bitter. "That's what one of the bosses called me, Little Black Sambo. Made me see red, but what could I do?"

"Nothing," Lime said.

"Might as well slit your own throat as argue with a white man then," Smith agreed. "I closed my eyes for the beating but it never came. I opened them to see Remy holding the man's arm, saying, 'Wanna hit someone, mon, hit me. I can use the exercise. I'm taking on the deputies Saturday night and did you get your bet down?' Smith shook his head. "Mr. Sunny Side Up started pulling out his money and Remy walked him away, motioned at me to git. So I got. That was the first time Knockout saved my life."

"More shrimp, Codell?" Catherine asked.

"No, thanks, need room for gumbo," Smith said. "Second time your father saved my life was what I said before, smothering the flames when I was burning alive. That led to the third time." He ate some gumbo, and his eyes grew wide. "Who made this?" he said.

"That would be me," Lucien said.

"Best I've ever tasted, and I've tasted it all over," Smith said. "It's just like your daddy used to make."

Lucien's eyebrows arched. "It's my own recipe, Codell. How's that possible?"

Smith shrugged. "In your DNA, I suppose. Remy taught me how to make it because the crew missed the taste of home."

"Dark roux?" Catherine said. "No tomato?"

"Yes, ma'am. Tomato was Creole, not Cajun. This tastes the same, I swear."

"Lord works in mysterious ways," Lucien said. "In men and gumbo."

Raider buttered a long crust of cornbread. "You were saying about the third time?"

"That grease burned me deep," Smith said. "Remy carried me to a lifeboat and put me in the only empty seat. Not without a little trouble, though."

"Grandpa liked trouble," Catherine smiled.

"Don't I know it," Smith said, laughing. "Loved him a good fight and making a tidy profit betting on himself. He said his fists were his savings plan for his boys."

"I wondered how he managed to buy you and Marcus new school clothes each year on an oil hand's wages," Catherine said. "And those nice Christmas presents."

Lucien turned his head. "Please continue, Codell," he

rasped. "Lifeboats and trouble?"

"At the boat, a racist boss by name of Bagley was kicking workers out of the way so he could grab the last seat." Smith's face darkened. "Old boy was a proper son of a bitch, excuse the French. He played favorites, took bribes for better shifts, sucked up to bosses but spit on workers. Saddled me with that Sambo nickname."

"What a jerk," Raider said.

Smith cackled. "Man got his, though. Remy told Bagley that I got hurt saving the lives of crewmen, so I was getting the last seat. Bagley was furious, said no Little Black Sambo was taking the place of a white man. Remy shoved him out of the way and put me in the boat. Bagley came at him with a knife and Knockout hit him hard as Joe Lewis. One punch, bam, lights out."

Everybody nodded, looking pleased.

"Then he told me something I won't forget even after I'm playing pinochle with the earthworms in my coffin," Smith said. "Remy said I was on that lifeboat because I had to fulfill my destiny."

"Your destiny?" Lucien said.

Smith nodded. "He called destiny 'a dream with a knockout punch' because nobody can stop you from fulfilling it. 'This lifeboat's your ticket to doing something special with your life,' he said. 'You have a destiny, Cookie, a dream. Go find it.'" He tapped his temple. "Something like that, anyway. I'm not as sharp as I used to be in rememberies."

"I sympathize, Codell," Lucien said, tapping his own temple.

"Remy lowered our lifeboat then dragged Bagley to another," Smith said, his voice husky as the memory relit. "Boss man was a viper, but Remy wouldn't let him burn. They both got in the boat, and then Remy bailed out like tigers on his tail. Yelled something about Pieton and Geronimo as he ran for the crane tower, which was on the other side of the deck." His compressed his lips in frustration. "Man would have been off that rig and home if he hadn't decided to rescue his best friend Pie."

"You'd escaped by then?" Lime asked.

Smith nodded. "My lifeboat was in the water and moving away, but Remy's voice cut the air like a foghorn. I heard him yelling about Pie using the Geronimo, which meant Pie was at the top of Knockout's derrick crane. Not much later, a series of explosions ripped through the rig. I knew Remy had *Stink Bug*, but I never knew if he made it inside."

"He did," Lucien said. "But he didn't." He explained.

Tears ran from Smith's eyes. "I got along with the white crew because everyone liked my cooking. But Remy Broussard? He didn't care about skin color. A car's engine was more important than its paint job, he said. No small thing in fifty-five." He looked at Lucien. "What I never understood was why."

"Why what?" Lucien asked.

"Why he treated me like a white man," Smith said. "Or, more accurately, why my blackness was irrelevant to his decisions. That's more the norm these days, but in the South in the fifties, it was unheard of." He looked around. "Or was the Louisiana of his youth a unicorn of love for all humankind?"

Lucien laughed. "Hardly. We had shits and saints just like anyone. My father was different because of this." He lifted a notebook. "Read the page I bookmarked."

"What is this?" Smith asked.

"A journal my father kept for me and my brother while he was on Happy Jack," Lucien said. "That page answers your question."

Smith read the note. He sat back, shook his head, and read it again.

"Dayum," he breathed.

"What I said when I read it," Lucien said. "That's why he had no problem putting you in that lifeboat, Codell, or offering you cigarettes."

"If it's not an imposition on family privacy, Lucien," Raider said. "I'd love to read that notebook."

Lucien nodded. "Thought you might. I made copies for all of you."

Smith stood, picked up his glass, and saluted the sky.

"Your father died a hero that day," he said. "But before that, he was the finest kind. When Mr. Lime tracked me down, I was honored to fly here to tell my story to his kin." He winked. "Riding in his jet and limo wasn't too shabby either."

"I had a dream," Lime said.

Raider fingered his head scar. "I had a dream . . . had, had, no, *have* a dream," he said. "I have a dream. Why do those words sound familiar? I mean, before now?"

"It's from the Martin Luther King speech," Underwood said. "'I have a dream that my four little children will one day live in a nation—'"

"'—where they will not be judged by the color of their skin but by the content of their character,'" Lucien said. "America's finest speech after the Gettysburg Address."

"Your father appreciates your kindness, Lucien," Smith said.

"Why would he appreciate such a thing?" Lucien wondered.

Smith refilled his glass. "I told Dr. King about Knockout and me at the lifeboat. He liked the story so much, it wound up in his 'Dream' speech."

Silence.

"You knew Martin Luther King?" Raider said.

"I worked for the man," Smith said.

"Codell Smith . . . you're *the* Codell Smith?" Underwood said. "Dr. King's communications director?"

Smith raised an eyebrow. "Assistant director, one of many, and not a big fish in any sense. How could you possibly know about me, Jennifer?"

"When I was a baby executive, I wrote press releases for Martin Luther King Day," she said. "I read his biographies and ran across your name a few times. How did you wind up working for Dr. King?"

Smith declined a fresh bowl of gumbo. "Remy told me to ride that lifeboat to a life that mattered. I took it seriously, working three jobs while going to college. I was a churchgoing man, then as now, and Mike was a guest minister one Sunday."

"Who's Mike?" Underwood asked.

"Martin Luther King. Friends and family called him Mike," Smith said, looking sheepish. "I'm sorry, I forget not everybody knows that."

"Mike," Underwood said. "That is so cool."

"Cool as snow in August," Smith said. "Anyway, I was so mesmerized by his sermon that after he moved into civil rights, I heard Knockout whispering in my ear, 'This is why I put you in that chariot. Go get you some.' I started doing volunteer work for the King operation. Couple years later, Mike hired me onto the professional staff." He tapped the table with his spoon. "The operation being penny-pinched, staff did whatever was needed any given day. When we were short of cooks, I picked up a fry pan."

"Shades of Happy Jack," Lucien said.

"I still like to cook," Smith said. "I was in the kitchen one day when Mike wandered in. I offered to fix him a meal and he said no, you sit, I'll cook. He raided the Frigidaire, made up a couple omelettes, and we talked, just him and me. One story led to another, and I told him your father's observation that destiny is a dream with a knockout punch. Mike was intrigued and asked for the context. I told him about the rig and blowout and me telling your father, 'I've got a destiny. I've got a dream,' as the lifeboat took me away."

"You served my father's words to Martin Luther King?" Lucien said.

Smith laughed. "In a way. But Mahalia Jackson made those words real."

"I know that name. She was famous even in the UK," Underwood said. "Sensational gospel singer."

"Nobody sang the Lord's spirit better," Smith agreed. "She was close with Mike and his wife Coretta, and she worked on the campaign. She's why 'I have a dream' made the speech at all."

"How so?" Raider asked.

Smith tilted his face to the sun, remembering. "The words 'I have a dream' weren't in the original speech. They hadn't been written, not by the speechwriters or by Mike. In the middle of his delivery, Mahalia was seized by the Spirit and called out, 'Tell them about the dream. Tell them about the dream!" Mike sensed a moment, switched to preacher cadence—he was so good at seamless oratory—and dropped the bomb: *I have a dream.* Four perfect words. But if not for Remy, they might not have been there at all."

"Much as I'd love to give my father credit," Lucien said, "he suggested that phrase in an entirely different context."

Smith nodded. "Don't get me wrong, Lucien, Mike came up with 'I have a dream' on his own. Man was brilliant at oratorical flourish, and he'd talked for years about his dreams for our people. He . . . and Remy . . ." He swallowed hard as he teared up.

"Go on, you're among friends," Lucien said.

Smith nodded. "To this day, I believe the Lord used Remy's decency to me to unchain Mike from the written script, which let him elevate a decent speech into one the world will remember forever. Four score and seven years ago. A date which will live in infamy. We few, we happy few, we band of brothers. I have a dream."

"I made him an offer he couldn't refuse," Lime deadpanned.

"What's even funnier," Smith said over the laughter, "is God worked this miracle through a fry cook."

"You done good, Cookie," Catherine said. "You and Grandpa Knocks."

Smith cleared his throat. "I knew the moment Mike said it that 'I have a dream' was my destiny. I needed to make it part of myself. My parents hadn't given me a middle name, and Mahalia's nickname was 'Halie.' I took Halie for my middle name to honor Mahalia, Martin, and Remy Broussard. Only my closest friends call me Halie. Please do."

Lucien jumped to his feet and flung open his arms. Smith grabbed him in a bear hug. They rocked and thumped backs while the rest of the table joined them, looking like a pile of crabs dancing around food.

"Thank you for this gift, Halie," Catherine said, eyes wet. "Dad and I always wondered about Grandpa's final hours. Now we know."

"He was my Cajun Martin Luther King." A mischievous smile creased his face. "For an opposing point of view, anybody interested in what happened to Bagley?"

Everyone nodded. Smith drank more lemonade. "The oil company promoted him to the mainland. He drove across the Midwest, supervising well installations. That was the perfect job for him because the Midwest was a hotbed of the KKK."

"Bagley was in the Klan?" Catherine asked.

"To peckerwoods like Bagley, a Ku Klux Klan outfit was the robe of Jesus," Smith said. "The man not only joined up, he got promoted to local Kleagle."

"Bet that made his mother proud," Lime muttered.

"I always assumed Bagley was hatched, not born," Smith said. "Anyway, he and his cutthroats were in their finest whites one night, splashing gasoline on a cross they'd planted in a black family's yard in southern Indiana. He didn't realize the wind had blown high-test back onto his robe and shoes, so when he fired up his Zippo . . ."

"Bagley barbecue," Lime said as everyone hooted. "And on that note, Lucien, I'm all out of surprises and ready to turn the gavel back to you."

Lucien motioned to the band, which resumed "When the

Saints Come Marching In." Catherine directed them to a path through the trees. They swayed to the funeral jazz, and when they turned a bend cloaked by a sprawling mangrove, they saw Remy's polished coffin atop a mossy tree stump. The coffin was crafted from cypress and sat pretty in the dappled sunshine, handrails gleaming like French horns. The band switched to the solemn hymn "In the Sweet By and By."

"Grandpa, meet Raider, Lime, Underwood, and your old friend Cookie Smith," Catherine said. "The rest of us you know." They swayed up to the coffin. Smith kissed the wood over Remy's face, whispered, "Thank you for my life, my friend," then grasped the handrail as others took their spots. The band played "Nearer My God To Thee" for the casket walk, and as they passed under the filigreed Broussard gate-topper to the family mausoleum at the back of the property, swung into "St. James Infirmary Blues."

"This ballad's moody as hell," Raider said. "But I always liked it."

"My father did too. He sang it whenever he worked in the yard," Lucien said. "It's about a nineteenth century British soldier visiting his dying battle comrade in the infirmary." He grinned. "Or a British soldier who stabbed a prostitute and reflected on his foul deed as she died in the infirmary. Lots of legends from which to choose."

Raider ran his finger along the casket, admiring Lucien's craftsmanship. "Speaking of legends, was it Cab Calloway who made the song famous?"

"Louis Armstrong made it a hit. Cab made it legendary by performing it in the Betty Boop cartoon Snow White."

"Betty Boop?" Raider said, raising an eyebrow. "Snow . . .

White?"

"Cab sang St. James Infirmary during Snow White's funeral. She laid in a casket made of ice, and Cab played a white-skinned Koko the Clown. Watching it stoned probably helped," Lucien said. "Anyway, the song is universal because the lyrics speak of death, *Take apart your bones and put 'em back together. Tell your momma that you're somebody new.* To me it conjures the spirits, ghosts, and hoodoos of the underworld. Perfect for today because that was one of my father's passions."

"Death?"

"Angels, spirits, and hoodoos."

Underwood wiped her humidity-dotted brow with a kerchief. "Why a mausoleum instead of six feet under, Catherine?" she asked.

"Above-ground burials are standard in the bayou," Catherine said. "The water table is high, so flooding and hurricanes force coffins out of the ground."

Lucien swept his arm through the air. "Imagine an entire city of the dead bobbing in a lake. That's what every cemetery would become if they were underground."

Underwood shivered.

"I know. I've witnessed that sadness and still can't shake it. That's why we bury our kin in God's clear air," Lucien said.

"Did you build this mausoleum?" Raider asked.

"Me and Parson and some neighborhood kids," Lucien said. "Louisiana allows family cemeteries, so we started stacking stone. I'll give you the grand tour."

They were ushered into the building, which Raider found surprisingly intimate for its spaciousness. Oversized cupboard doors lined its left and right walls. The back wall displayed black-and-white family photographs, under which was a table shrouded in purple velvet. Framed paintings of sugar skulls, those riotously decorated human skulls that represented the departed souls in the circle of life, hung from beige stone walls. A crystal chandelier provided illumination.

"The doors cover the burial chambers?" Raider said.

"Yes. Each chamber is large enough for a full-size coffin. Along with urns, keepsakes, whatever else you want to put inside," Lucien said, patting the door closest to him. "My father goes here in the middle, above Amélie and below my brother Marcus. Both of my late wives, Joanne and Molly, are on the opposite wall. I'll join them when it's my turn. I left plenty of room for Catherine and any family she might have someday. They can join us if they want."

"Of course we want," Catherine said.

Lucien patted his daughter's cheek. "But she's too young and pretty to worry about death. That's for us old-timers."

"Family forever, la meilleure," Raider said.

"Me, no, not a la meilleure, me," Lucien said, waving it away. "I know one when I see one, that's all." He heard a car honk and looked out the door. A barrel-shaped man with a porkpie hat was emerging from a sedan. His attire was somber but not priestly. His legs bowed as he walked. Everyone filed out and gathered around the coffin. When the man reached the group, he kissed Catherine's cheek.

"I'm so happy you made it," she said.

"Me too," Parson Dumont said. "Think I should hug the old guy?"

"He'd like that, even though he won't say so," she said, dark eyes glittering.

Dumont wrapped Lucien in a bear hug, then kissed the top of his head. "It's your lucky day. You get smooched without buying me dinner first."

"Not enough money in the world to pay for your dinners," Lucien said as he patted Dumont's ample belly.

"Show some respect, Nicotine," Dumont said, pretend-pouting. "I'm your man of the cloth."

"Come again?" Lucien said.

"Your preacher woke up with the flu," Dumont said. "He says he tried to call you."

"I didn't hear the phone," Lucien said. "We had our hands full."

"I can imagine," Dumont said. "Anyway, he called me. He was crushed he couldn't officiate your old man's funeral. I said hey, I'm a Parson, I'll do it."

"Parson's your name, not your profession."

"Wrong, gumbo breath. I'm a mail-order minister," Dumont said, pulling a folded sheet of paper from his jacket. "This here's from the Church of the Holy Mofo. Cost me ten bucks and worth every penny."

"Jesus wept," Lucien said, rolling his eyes. He introduced the rest, then said, "This hombre is Parson Dumont."

"The aforementioned Mr. Dumont?" Underwood said.

"The same, madame. We were homicide detectives in New Orleans until the city decided it no longer required our, um, services."

Dumont grinned. "That's a lot nicer than they put it when they kicked us out."

"You said it. Anyway, I joined Fish and Game and he became a private investigator. Parson remains my best friend and le meilleure—"

"Dad-speak for 'the very best,'" Catherine reminded.

"—despite my constant sorrow over the mischief he gets me into because he just can't help himself."

"Without me, Nicotine," Dumont said, "your life would be dull as fish drool."

"You say that like it's a bad thing," Lucien said. "Didn't you have an important stakeout today?"

"They're all important."

"Sure, be delusional. How'd you get out of it?"

Dumont cleared his throat. "A charming young lady with an affection for private eyes asked me to show her the ways of my world. I invited her to today's stakeout. She brought fatty snacks. I think I'm in love." He grinned. "She knows her way around a videocam, so I left her to keep an eye on things. She'll send a live feed if she needs me."

Lucien tilted his head. "You sure, Parson? We can handle this. Don't let me mess up your work."

"I put on nice clothes," Dumont protested.

"Your socks do match," Lucien said.

"I also wrote a homily, and I'm not gonna deprive you of the magnificence of my preaching. Let's give Big Daddy the sendoff he deserves. But first, let's do the thing."

"The thing?" Lime said.

Lucien nodded. "The thing. Follow me, if you please."

They trooped back into the mausoleum. Lucien switched on a spotlight aimed at the family photos and purple shroud. He faced the gathering.

"I wanted this to go into the chamber with my father. But like the man, it doesn't fit in tight spaces, so here it stays." He pulled away the shroud in a single motion.

A replica of *Stink Bug* glowed orange in the light.

Raider blinked. "Wow. That's not how I remember it looking."

"Seven decades under water, I wouldn't be dewy fresh either," Dumont said. "Lucien donated the original to a maritime museum that will display it as the first successful prototype of today's oil rig escape pods. But first he asked an artist to create a three-foot replica for the mausoleum. She carved it from mahogany and here we are."

"Once in a while you have a good idea," Lucien said.

"They're all good."

"Said nobody, ever," Lucien said.

"It's lovely," Underwood said, opening the miniature hatch.

"It's a ship in a bottle," Lucien said. "See my father and his belongings inside? I don't know how Rebecca managed it other than magic. It will stay on the table, under the photographs, as part of the family history." He pointed at Raider. "A replica of the plaque Mr. Pieton attached to *Stink Bug* is there on the wall. Please go read it, Captain Raider."

"No need, I remember what it said," Raider said.

"I believe you might have overlooked something."

"Huh." Raider walked over and peered at the plaque.

USS Stink Bug
Constructed by Pieton's
unskilled assistant Knockout
Oil Rig Happy Jack
1955 AD

Brought home to Remy Broussard's family
by Raider, Lime, and Underwood

Made pretty by Nicotine's
unskilled assistant Dumont

Lime, Smith, and Underwood crowded in to read. Lime opened his mouth, then closed it without words. Underwood patted his back.

"You're going to have to do something about these pollen allergies if we're going to visit again, Lucien," Raider said, eyes bright in the floodlight.

"Right after I add Halie to the plaque," Lucien said. "Welcome to the family, all of you. Now let's do my father right."

They shuffled outside and joined hands around the coffin. Marigolds scented the humid breeze, which ruffled the phlox and flowering tobacco that picture-framed the mausoleum. Lucien, Catherine, and Dumont read from Remy's notebook. Underwood, Raider, Lime, and Smith thanked them for the opportunity to close the circle that started in Morocco, dove deep to a leaking well cap, crossed paths with two doomed oil rigs in two separate centuries, embraced Martin Luther King, Mahalia Jackson, dreams, destinies, fighting, barbecue, angels, and hoodoos, and ended with friends in the final resting place of a giant. Dumont led them in "Amazing Grace" then broke out a Mason jar of apple pie moonshine. He splashed shine into tumblers and raised his over the cypress coffin.

"To Lucien's father," Dumont said. "Once lost, now found, together forever."

"To my father," Lucien said. "Who did the best he knew how for his family, and therefore remains the best father I ever had."

"To my grandfather," Catherine said. "A good man and only grandpa I ever had."

"To Mister Broussard," Smith said. "Who gave his life that I might live."

"To Remy Broussard," Raider, Underwood, and Lime said.

"To Knockout Broussard," Dumont said, unfolding the lined yellow paper on which he'd scratched his homily at the stakeout. "Who took the long way to Heaven, and when he arrived, God said, 'Welcome home, my son, it's been a minute, right?' and Remy replied as he hopped off his scorched chariot, 'It sure has, Lord, it'll be nice to be warm and dry after all those years in the drink, and what do I owe you to garage my ride?' and God replied, 'Heroes park for free.'"

"Amen," everyone said.

18

Isle of Skye, Scotland

"Lucien rescued Catherine from a shipwreck?" Underwood said as she slipped under the bedsheets to rest her brown curls on Raider's chest of tangles. The croft house was chilly damp, so she'd lit the wood-burning stove. It made the bedroom toasty, with overtones of smoke and peat. "Near the house in Thibodaux?"

Raider nodded. "When she was a baby, a boat smuggling immigrants into the United States broke apart in the bayou during a storm." He paused to pour Jen a dram of the Port Ellen whisky they'd uncapped at supper. "Parish sheriff's dispatch called Lucien because he lived nearby. Lucien hopped in his fast-boat and hightailed it out to the crash site. He found the baby, no one else."

"Oh, no," Underwood said. "How many died?"

"Fifteen, including captain and mate," Raider said. "Coast Guard told Lucien that everyone else had been pinned in the wreckage. Nobody had IDs and the pilot didn't file a flight plan." Saying the story aloud made his face tighten. "Authorities had no way to track down the girl's family, so Lucien and his wife raised her."

"Which wife?"

"The first, Joanne," he said. "When the baby became old

enough to understand, Lucien asked her to join his family. She became Catherine Broussard."

Underwood sighed. "That's lovely."

"And you a hard-boiled oil baroness," he said.

"That's just business," she said, clinking her crystal to his. "I'm a sucker for romance stories. Take Remy and Amélie. He never gave up hope they'd reunite, and one day, it happened." She made a face. "It did take both of them dying horribly, so call it a love story by the Coen brothers."

"I know another love story," Raider said.

"Oh, boy," Underwood said, putting down the whisky.

He reveled at his fortune in attracting such a marvelous woman. *Don't fuck this up,* he recalled Underwood saying to him about the well cap. He didn't then, he wouldn't now.

She pushed the sheet to her knees, smiling as he sucked in his breath. She'd never been with a man who reacted to her with such primal animal passion. She liked it. "Speaking of love story, I'm glad you finally caught my drift, Raider," she said. "All the hints I was putting down. I thought I was going to have to draw you a map."

"I was saving the world," Raider said. "Sorry if I didn't have time to pick up on your fancy little clues."

"Then allow me to demonstrate, show pony," she said, kicking the green silk sheet to the floor to show nothing but her birthday suit. She slipped the solid-gold Super Bowl ring off her finger, put it on the bed table, and kissed him until all engines lit. Raider pushed them both into high rev, then announced he was diving for buried treasure. He talked to her body as he hunted, saying something about a sea creature with yellow gonads. That struck her as so Raiderly she started to laugh, but a bellowed "moo" interrupted.

He looked up. "I hope that's Scottish for 'yes, yes, oh God, yes.'"

She burst out laughing. "It's Gracie. She's outside our window. She wants treats."

"Go away, Gracie," Raider said. "All my treats are for Lady Jen."

Silence.

"Did someone mention treats?" Underwood whispered.

"Indeed," Raider said, snuggling back into her body and launching his probe. An hour later they rolled away from each other, panting and pale. Raider's back and arms twitched from exertion. He thought about all he'd gone through in the Gulf, which led to Underwood, which led to this.

"I've one more thimble of methane," he said. "If you're not fresh out of oil."

She blew out her breath. "I dunno, Raider, you might have played out Underwood Prospect." She slowly kissed him chest to lips, then propped herself over his body to study his hazel eyes and lightly stubbled face. She felt him stir against her leg.

"Damn the torpedoes," she said with a shiver. "Full speed ahead."

Raider complied, then after a while managed to gasp, "Thar she blows."

She kissed him to breathlessness.

"Everyone's a poet, la meilleure," she said.

REMY'S NOTEBOOK

A 'Knockout' Diary
For My Boys

Written by Their Proud Father,
Remy "Knockout" Broussard

1

ello, Lucien and Marcus. I bought this notebook and pencil in New Orleans so I could write down things for you. I'm away from home for months at a time, and I know it affects you. Boys need their father. But I'm working hard to put food on our table and pay our bills, and that means I have to be here three months at a stretch. I promise to make it up to you best I can when I'm home. I hope you understand. Meantime, this notebook will record what I think so you can read it someday and make fun of your old man.

2

ello, Lucien and Marcus. My oil rig is called the Happy Jack. It's owned by Derringer Oil of Texas. I don't know if Jack is happy, but I am. (Ha! Good one, Knock!) I like this crew except for the boss, whose name is Bagley but we call him Dirtbag because he is. The food is good, particularly when made by a young man we call Cookie—because he's a cook. I will teach him to make my gumbo because it will remind me of home and you.

3

ello, Lucien and Marcus. You'll have to learn Cajun French to read this because your father's written English is terrible. Get good grades in English if you want to be successful.

4

ello, Lucien and Marcus. The Cold War is getting hotter. I heard on the radio the Pentagon is planning to build nuclear missiles that can reach Moscow or Red China. They call them "ICBMs." I wish they wouldn't do this because, people being people, someone will panic and push the button and blow us all to smithereens for no good reason. I hope President Eisenhower keeps the cool head he showed us GIs in Europe during the war. Ike is a good man. I saw him once at an Army base in France. He waved at me. I saluted him. A fine moment, that.

5

*H*ello, Lucien and Marcus. We listen to baseball games when we're not pumping oil. (We fixed an antenna to the top of the crane, then ran a wire from it to the radio. It pulls in so many stations we could probably hear ball games from Mars. I wonder what kind of games Martians play? If it's baseball and they have more than two hands, do they put a glove on each one? These are the things your father thinks about when he can't sleep.) Maybe when I'm home we can build a baseball field in the backyard. Any ball you hit into the swamp will be a home run because if you run in to fetch it, a gator will bite your butt. I'd hate to have to swab iodine down there. Stinky. Ha!

6

*H*ello, Lucien and Marcus. The Syracuse Nationals won the NBA title by beating the Fort Wayne Pistons. Pretty good ball game, though I didn't get to hear the whole thing, I was mudding pipes.

7

ello, Lucien and Marcus. Your mother, Amélie, will come home one day. I'm sad she left us, but you have to understand she's young and not thinking straight. I made such mistakes when I was young, but I got passed them and she will too because she loves us so much.

8

ello, Lucien and Marcus. More about your mother, Amélie. When she realizes how much she misses you and me, she will call us and I will drive to wherever she is and fetch her home. Please keep the house tidy so if she shows up without telephoning, she will be pleased at how well you've been raised.

9

ello, Lucien and Marcus. That big Disneyland fun park opened in California. When I get some time off from the rigs, I'll take you two boys and Mom too if she's home by then. I hear you get to meet Mickey Mouse. Do you think Mickey would like your old man? If not, I'll stand way back so he's not scared to play with you.

10

ello, Lucien and Marcus. Hoo-ha, what a thunderstorm we had last night. So much lightning. A bolt hit the crane I operate, so my best friend Pieton and I had to fix it today. It was a mess, but Pie is a genius with tools and so we got the job done.

11

ear Lucien and Marcus. Pie told circus stories and we all cracked up laughing. You would like him even though he is short and dumb. (I added that part so I could read it to him, ha!) Before the war, he was an acrobat with his brothers, and they walked on high wires and flew on flying trapezes. They toured to many cities like Tallahassee, Mobile, and even Boston. He was shot in the ankle by a Nazi in World War Two, so he couldn't fly high anymore. He is now a great mechanic and we work the same shift on Happy Jack. He is a good amigo. Even if he is balder than a cue ball. Ha again!

12

*D*ear Lucien and Marcus. At night I smoke cigarettes and look at the stars. I tried counting them once and gave up at one thousand and fifty-two. Pie told me there are a trillion. I can't even imagine that number. I wonder if Star Workers stand on Star Oil Decks and look at us and wonder about the same things we do.

13

*H*ello, Lucien and Marcus. I know you boys won't believe it, but it's hot and humid here today! Ha! More soon because I have to go to work pumping oil so the yellow bus can take you to school.

14

Dear Lucien and Marcus. One of the workers I share cigarettes with some nights is black. He is sixteen, I think, and works as a fry cook. He is a pleasant young man, and veery smart. Once he asked me why I was decent to the black crew when I am white. (As you know, my skin is as dark as chewing tobacco, but because I'm a Cajun I'm considered a white man. No, I don't know why, either. Race things are strange.) I told Cookie—that's what we call both our cooks, Cookie—the paint job of a car doesn't make it run good or bad, the engine does. He liked that.

15

Dear Lucien and Marcus. I thought more about what Cookie asked me. Before the war, I thought poorly of black men. I considered them lazy, untrustworthy, and so dumb as to be retarded. Then I was a machine gunner at the Battle of the Bulge. As a U.S. Army infantryman I ground many Nazis into deathwurst. I was good at it, though I didn't enjoy it as others seemed to. Anyway, during one battle I was stabbed through the left lung by a Nazi. The man's skin was white as snow and he had blue eyes. I killed him dead with my Colt .45, but the stab collapsed my lung and I was suffocating. An American medic crawled under fierce German machine gun fire to fix me. That man was black as a licorice stick and had dark eyes. He dragged me to a foxhole under intersecting streams of bullets. To push me over the edge of the foxhole he had to raise himself up a little bit. When he did that he caught a hail of bullets. I saw him die in a splatter of blood. He looked surprised. I felt bad for him, and for his family who would no longer enjoy his presence. After that, I decided skin color made no difference to a man's heart because a white man nearly kilt me and a black man saved my life. I was wrong to think them lazy and stupid, and decided racism is just a way for politicians and some preachers to get rich. They should live in foxholes and get stabbed by Mauser bayonets before they get to serve in government. They would change their tune.

16

ear Lucien and Marcus. Did our house make it through the hurricane? I heard on the news that Lafourche Parish got flooded good but that our area was all right. I built that house out of cypress wood because it's strong and resists water and all those insects hate it. If there was any damage, write it down and I will fix it when I get home.

17

ear Lucien and Marcus. I hope the school clothes fit and you like them. By the time I get home you probably will have outgrown them and I will buy you somme more. We will keep the clothing store man in business with all the clothes you two will need as you grow, you.

18

*D*ear Lucien and Marcus. I heard on the radio President Ike is sending "military advisers" to a little country called Vietnam, which is next door to Red China. Half of Vietnam likes freedom the same as us, the other likes Communism. The Communists are trying to take over the freedoms of the others and so they're fighting a war. I hope you boys don't have to serve in Vietnam when you grow up. Europe was hard enough and it doesn't have those nasty hot jungles. We had hedgerows and those were tough, but there were no tigers or malarias. I hope the Vietnams settle their hash soon.

19

ear Lucien and Marcus. The black people in the South are tired of being shoved around by white people, and they're not going to take it lying down anymore. A girl aged fifteen got on a public bus in Montgomery, Alabama, and sat down. When white people got on later, the driver told the black girl to give up her seat to the whites and move to the back. The girl said no, that she paid the same ticket fare as them so she was staying put. Police came and put her in jail, but she still refused to say she was wrong. After her daddy brought her home, he loaded his shotgun and stood guard at their house all night in case the white hoods of the KKK men showed up. The Klan are bullies and I wish they'd burn themselves up when they light their crosses on fire. I admire this girl for standing up for herself because I don't like being shoved around either. Don't you let anyone bully you, boys. If they do, warn them once to knock it off or else. Look stern so they know you're serious. If they keep pushing you, punch them until they bleed. Only then will they leave you alone. Never start a fight, boys, but always finish it. Otherwise everyone and their uncle picks on you.

20

*D*ear Lucien and Marcus. Wars are stupid. Working men like us get killed, but nothing changes. Well, except for the people who build things for war—they get rich as Vanderbilts and Rockerfellas. When the war is over, they throw whatever they didn't use into the oceans so everyone thinks they ran out, then start another war and get richer. If your country asks you to fight, you will do so, because that's what Americans do, fight for our country. But don't think you're fighting for a noble cause. You're fighting to make rich men richer. That is how the world works.

21

*D*ear Lucien and Marcus. Oil rigs are supposed to have enough lifeboats for every man on the crew. Happy Jack does, but just barely. There is only one seat per worker, which doesn't account for accidents, fires, or other losses of boats in an emergency like a typhoon. I decided to make an escape pod that can survive any storm or fire and also be watertight if I have to abandon ship. (During an abandon-ship drill, of course! We never have emergencies on oil rigs, so you don't have to worry about your father getting hurt on the job. I will always come home to you, I promise.)

22

*D*ear Lucien and Marcus. I know your mother, Amélie, will telephone the house any day now to say she's sorry she run away and could she come home. You tell her of course she can, and if I'm on the Happy Jack when she calls, she should take a taxicab from wherever she is and come home. I put money in an envelope to pay for the taxicab, and you boys can find it in my sock drawer.

23

*D*ear Lucien and Marcus. The escape pod is coming along nicely. The boys nicknamed it Stink Bug because it looks like one of those VW Beetle cars in America now. You have seen those roundy-top things, I hope? Anyway, I salvaged a good-sized bronze pipe from a Navy ship to use as the main body. I found the pipe on a garbage scow filled with worn-out and broken military equipment. The scow was sailing into the Gulf to dump the scrap. The pipe is forty-eight inches wide and ninety-six inches long, and both ends are threaded for caps. It will be dandy to sit in. I bought the fitting and caps for three dollars, and the junkman was happy because he was going to throw them overboard anyway. I also bought a hatch from a torpedoed submarine, and I'll figure out how to attach it to the top so I can get in and out of the pipe. Also, I'll need some pontoons for the bottom of the boat. Without them that big pipe will sink to the bottom and I'll be eaten by whales and come out the other end as whale poop, which will be a good time to sing St. James Infirmary. Ha! Don't worry, nothing can kill your father, who is Knockout. I will be home to shake your hands soon, I promise.

24

ear Lucien and Marcus: I whooped eleven sheriff's deputies in a fight in New Orleans. That's a new record. I like police officers, so I don't hurt 'em none when we fight. They enjoy fighting me back because it's more fun than writing tickets. When I leave the rigs someday, maybe I'll be a real boxer even though I wasn't quite good enough before now. Sugar Ray Broussard? Cajun Knockout? You boys think of a fun nickname that would look good on the back of a shirt and we'll sew ourselves some jim-dandies when I get home. Your father can't wait to see you two.

25

ear Lucien and Marcus: Did I tell you my friends christened my escape pod *Stink Bug?* I don't remember so I'll tell you again here. Those peckerwoods! Ha! It's because they think it looks like those new VW Beetle cars they're selling. I can't buy a Beetle car because they're so tiny my legs won't fit, but maybe your mother would like one. I doubt small cars will ever catch on, since Americans love big Detroit iron and that will never change. And with gasoline so cheap at a dime a gallon, why wouldn't you ride around in big-car style?

26

ear Lucien and Marcus. I watch wildlife from the deck. The birds are very friendly even if they poop on our heads sometimes. They ride the wind currents and come down to visit when I put treats in my hands. Big schools of fish swim by the rig, and dolphins jump like those Olympics fellows. Pie and I seen a whale the other day—thar she blows! I like animals more than some people, because animals never hurt you for stupid reasons, whereas some people hurt you for fun. "Whereas." Pie taught me that word. He said I should put fancier words in my notes so you learn them. So use "whereas" sometimes so people think you're Fancy.

27

*D*ear Lucien and Marcus. My labors on my little submarine, *Stink Bug*, continues. I painted waterproof sealant on the threads, screwed on the end caps, and then welded the seams where the cap met the pipe. Each weld is perfect, like an unending caterpillar. I am proud of my welding skill, which Pie taught me. I cut a hole in the top of the pipe to let me get inside, and then welded the watertight submarine hatch over it. Then I attached pontoons to the bottom to keep my little Stinky afloat. I dropped the whole thing in the Gulf overnight and found there were no leaks the next morning. So far, so good. I am drawing *Stink Bug* and its parts in the back of this notebook. When I'm a famous boxer someday you can brag to your friends I also invented a floaty boat.

28

*D*ear Lucien and Marcus. Today I lined *Stink Bug*'s inside walls and floor with rubber in case the waves bounce me around when I'm inside. I added a seat, five-gallon water can, cylinder of compressed air so I can breathe when the hatch is dogged down—that means tightened and locked into place—a pee bucket, and an ammo box from a Ma Deuce to store this notebook. It's got a gasket so it's waterproof. A Coast Guard officer who was visiting the rig liked my idea so much he got me a government certificate that proves I invented it. Me, an inventor! I also got a contract to work on it for the government. My boss, Bagley, says he should get some of the credit because he let me work on it, but I told him no, that money is for my boys and besides, I did all the work on my time off. You remember my talking about Bagley, right? Don't ever be like that man. He is a grubby little dictator and he hates black people and he probably will be a Number One Klansman someday. He is a jerk, don't ever be his way. Enough about him. When I get home, I will bury the money that came with the *Stink Bug* contract next to the stump in the yard by the barbecue. In case you ever need money in an emergency, you can dig it up and there you are.

29

*D*ear *Lucien and Marcus.* Derringer Oil, which owns the Happy Jack, liked the idea of the escape pod too, and said I can continue to test it as much as I want when I'm not on shift. It was thoughtful of them, although I think they agreed because the government gives them money too, and so I am doing that. They called my work a "prototype," whatever that means. Your father is proud of his big little boat. Hey, I made a funny.

30

ear Lucien and Marcus. My boss, Bagley, the jerk, made me climb a rope up the side of the rig today to get from the tugboat to the deck. It smelled like a horse's butt. Not the boss, the rope, but come to think of it, Boss Bagley smells that way too. Ha! When you're grown, work for someone you respect. Sometimes you're stuck with Boss Bagleys, but when you have a choice, work for the best person you can find, or for yourself. If you work for yourself, you do all the chores, but you also keep all the profits, and the only person who gets to yell at you for being lazy is you. It's a very pretty day here in the Gulf, despite Bagley's stinky rope. The sky is blue and there are few clouds. The humidity isn't too high, a miracle. A supply tug delivered fifty pounds of bacon at three a.m. this morning and Cookie's frying a bunch for the fellas. I told you about Cookie, right, the young black man who cooks so well and is nice to everyone? He does bacon right, crispy till the ends turn up like a smile, but not burnt. I eat them in a pool of maple syrup. When I get home, I'll make fifty pounds for my favorite bacon boys in the whole world. I can't wait till we're together again.

ACKNOWLEDGEMENTS

No writer is an island, no writer stands alone. At least I don't. So, I'm proud to thank these good folks for helping me get this book out of my head and into your hands:

Britin Haller, my story editor, and what an editor! She found a crucial plot error in my original draft that, if not reworked, would have made me a bonehead to anyone who knows how human bones react to ocean water. She suggested the perfect fix, along with the idea of creating a tiny escape pod—"you know, like the astronauts use"—to get Remy Broussard off the burning rig. Then she tightened some scenes and enhanced others, all of which proves that behind every good writer is a great editor. An ocean of thanks, Brit.

Victoria Canzonetta, whose father was a Navy fighter pilot, and who served as a paramedic, divemaster, and protocol officer on a 204-foot superyacht. While at sea, she survived both a pirate attack and a typhoon, and her expertise boosted the realism of my nautical scenes. I salute you, Torry.

John Paine of John Paine Editorial Services, who copyedited the final (and factually correct) version into the flowing jazz every story needs to be worthy of readers.

Bill Page, the beta reader for all my novels and the man I call The Manuscript Whisperer for his relentless checking of times, dates, places, historical references, foreign words, movie titles, and other things I assert as Trvth. As always, Bill, much obliged.

Terri Lynn Coop, one of the best writers I know, who graciously agreed to serve as my second beta reader and, when finished, said it did not suck. High praise in writer world.

Erin Mitchell of HEW Communications, who formatted this book for hardcover, paperback, and e-book so the choice would be yours, then orchestrated the marketing plan that got the attention of so many readers and reviewers. Thanks for everything, Erin.

JT Lindroos, the artist who created the magnificent front and back covers that grace this book. Täydellinen!

Madeira James of Xuni design, who created my new website. Ain't it a peach?

ABOUT SHANE GERICKE

Shane Gericke earned the right to sing the blues, having survived a knife to his throat, a lightning strike, the death of his wife, and a pulmonary embolism the size of a Buick. But the quality of his voice suggested to him he was better off sticking to words and images.

Accordingly, he became the bestselling author of *Blown Away* (Debut Mystery of the Year, RT Book Reviews), *Torn Apart* (finalist, Thriller Award), and other crime novels, as well as winning international honors (Monochrome Awards and the National Wildlife Federation) for his landscape photography.

Before jumping into those fields, Gericke (pronounced YER-key) spent 25 years as a newspaper editor and writer, most prominently at the *Chicago Sun-Times*. While there he chaired the Chicago Newspaper Guild, and later in book world, chaired the ThrillerFest literary conference in Manhattan. He is a founding member of International Thriller Writers and a longtime member of Mystery Writers of America. He wanted to be Napoleon Solo, but the closest he ever got was Eagle Scout.

The lifelong Chicago resident recently turned in his snowblower for the hot desert winds of Arizona. Read more about him at ShaneGericke.com.

You can browse and buy his photographs at FineArtAmerica.

PRAISE FOR AUTHOR

Shane Gericke at his finest! OCEAN OF BONES is wholly absorbing and hard driving. Put on the coffee pot, because you'll want to stay up late to finish this gem.

GRANT BLACKWOOD, NO. 1 NEW YORK TIMES BESTSELLING AUTHOR

A first-rate cops-and-psychos novelist. His plucky heroine evokes the spirit of Thomas Harris' Clarice Starling.

PUBLISHER'S WEEKLY

One of the most remarkable thrillers I've read in a long time. Shane Gericke's twenty-five years in the newspaper world make every scene resonate with a you-are-there authenticity, as if I'm reading fact, not fiction. His characters feel remarkably real, also vivid, likeable, and compelling. I want to spend more and more time with them. Every scene has an intensity that made me turn the pages faster. The action is state-of-the-art. Pay attention—this one's a winner.

DAVID MORRELL, NO. 1 NEW YORK TIMES BESTSELLING AUTHOR, CREATOR OF RAMBO

Gericke's writing is a blistering rush of sheer artistry.

KEN BRUEN, BESTSELLING AUTHOR

An A-grade thriller by a Grade A writer. Shane Gericke is the real deal.

NO. 1 NEW YORK TIMES BESTSELLING AUTHOR, CREATOR OF JACK REACHER

A no-nonsense thriller, action-packed and explosive. A real page-turner!

ERICA SPINDLER, NEW YORK TIMES BESTSELLING AUTHOR

A rambunctious, devious novel full of chutzpah, high energy, and surprises. Forget roller coaster; this one reads like a rocket.

JOHN LUTZ, USA TODAY BESTSELLING AUTHOR

A shotgun start, an Indy 500 wild ride, and an explosive finish.

RT BOOK REVIEWS

Gericke is an expert in provoking suspense with horror, surpassing that of a Stephen King or Dean Koontz.

WHO DUNNIT MYSTERY MAGAZINE

A roller-coaster ride of a suspense thriller, and not for the faint of heart.

SUSPENSE MAGAZINE

Cat-and-mouse at its finest.

ALEX KAVA, NEW YORK TIMES BESTSELLING AUTHOR